MAJORCA MAC

By Vincent Rhomberg

DEDICATION AND ACKNOWLEDGEMENTS

This book is dedicated to my friend, "Mac,"
and my father, Edward D. Rhomberg.

All situations and characters in the story are fictional.
Any similarities to actual persons are coincidental.

Vincent Rhomberg
4428 Chippewa St.
St. Louis, MO 63116
vincentsiuc@yahoo.com

My special thanks to the friends who helped shape this book
by their comments, conversations and care:
Del Watlington, Jackie Compton, Constance Ruppender,
Jim Lambert, Leslie A Brown, Dana Winter. John MacEnulty
and Connie MacEnulty.

———

PROLOGUE
Unfinished Business

It was that damned envelope. If he had never found that envelope, everything would be as it was, as it had been for so many years, safe, solid, and smooth. But he did find it, and now things were different. Now his mind was filled with unfinished business.

The man sat at his desk in his office in New Jersey. He was there, but he wasn't working. He was staring. That was not normal. For years, every working day started the same. He arrived at his office, set down his briefcase, and hung his jacket carefully on the back of the visitor's chair opposite him. He could have placed his coat in the closet, there were hangers and plenty of space, but he liked it there, on the chair. It was ready in an instant if needed, and it gave a shirtsleeve feel to his work. Today, the jacket had not been placed with precision care. It was thrown haphazardly at the target. Yesterday, half of the suitcoat slid down the vinyl and was draping onto the floor.

After situating the jacket, the man fixed himself a cup of coffee. His secretary would have been happy to fetch the brew, but he liked to prepare the cup himself. By making the eye-opener, he got the coffee just the way he wanted it, with only himself to blame if it didn't satisfy. It wasn't only the quest for the perfect cup that prompted him; it was the ritual. He liked the way the coffee marked the beginning of his workday. To him, that cup was a start. A fresh cup, a fresh start. But yesterday, he hadn't filled the coffee to the proper brim line. Several times, he asked his secretary, Susie, why the coffee was so sweet. The day before, he carried the full cup with such imbalance, he left a line of droplets on the office floor, from the urn to the door.

Everyone at the office, some more quickly than others, noticed that something was not right. And of course, they all guessed as to what was bothering him. He had taken up drinking. He had a gambling problem. He was having an affair. They had all guessed, but none of them had guessed correctly.

On a typical day, he'd take a sip from his cup of ritual and then jump into action, checking email and organizing the day's work. That was his procedure. That was his practice. In his world, his office was his haven, and routine was his sanctuary. But for the past month, there was no haven. He could find no sanctuary. He sat there distracted. To a casual observer, his morning looked the same, but it wasn't.

The inbox on his desk, which was always neat, was overtaken by papers. Orders, contracts, mail, and proposals spilled from the bin, cascading onto the surface of his desk. And although each was a treasure to explore, a possibility for profit, the papers sat untouched. They were that way for several weeks. It wasn't only the clutter and the lack of alchemy that caused him concern. Lately, he realized he was staring, staring into space. At what, he was uncertain. But each day, it was becoming more and more difficult for him to keep his mind on business. He was preoccupied. It began with the discovery of that damned envelope and the photograph it contained.

Shake it off, he thought, get to work. He selected a proposal from the inbox and set it on his desk. He picked up his pen and began to review the document, but he didn't make it far. After a few minutes, he realized he was looking at the same sentence over and over. Whatever content and import it contained eluded him. He stopped, threw down his pen, and walked to the window.

Maybe it was his age, he thought. Middle-age is tricky. Youth is in the past, and retirement is not yet in the future's forefront. The present. That was the key. Stay in the present and be happy. Until a few weeks ago, it was easy. The past stayed in its place. Now the past was seeping into the present.

This happens to everyone, he thought. In younger years you are excited and eager. You are busy making a life; you don't think about the before. And then there comes a time when the past and the present meet, and you must choose the future. That is what was happening with him. He was thinking, wondering, and revisiting . . . thinking of the past, wondering about the present, and revisiting loose ends, trying to choose.

He thought all evidence of that part of his life was vanquished. He went through great efforts to make sure that all connections between then and now evaporated. That they were not just hidden but dissolved. And they were, as far as he knew, until he found that box. It was simple. He was looking through the closet, saw the box, and wondered what was in it. He didn't know it was Pandora's. He opened the box and discovered the envelope it contained. Curious, he opened the envelope and freed the photograph. That one photograph, that single image, engulfed him and consumed him, reminding him that the past was not gone. It did not evaporate. It was not dissolved. It was only hiding, waiting to be found. And now he was confronted by loose ends, devoured by loose ends that he wanted to tie; loose ends like finding an old double-crosser and settling an old debt. Not because he thought he could even the score; he didn't even know if there was anything to gain. He just wanted to close the books. It's one of the bad habits of his being in business; profit or loss, either way, he was happiest when the accounts were resolved. Unfinished business nagged and nagged and nagged at him, until it was settled. It did in his work, and it did in his life.

There was one piece of unfinished business he was reminded of by that picture. When he opened that envelope, the memory lashed out at him like a machete. It cut at him ever since. He spent a lot of time considering what he wanted to do. He finally decided. He didn't want to wait any longer. He didn't want the unfinished business to continue to occupy his waking moments. Today he would act.

The man at the desk opened a drawer. The envelope with the photo sat in that drawer, but he did not reach for it. Instead, he took out a business card he had placed there and dialed the number printed on it. After a few rings, a discrete voice answered. "Bradbury Investigations."

"Yeah, hello. I got your card from a golf-buddy of mine, Phil Kenzie."

"Yes?" the man on the phone said.

"You helped him a while back."

"I remember."

"I have a situation," the man at the business in New Jersey said.

"O.K. I'm listening."

"I want you to find someone."

"That shouldn't be too difficult," the investigator said.

4

"The guy's disappeared."

"Everyone is someplace."

"Yes, and I want to find where that is. The man built himself a boat a few years back and has been sailing around the world since."

"People leave traces. Boats too.

"We'll see. This guy does a great vanishing act."

"When's the last time you heard from him?"

"Twenty-five years ago. He's been gone for twenty-five years. We have some unfinished business. And I want to find him."

———————

CHAPTER 1
The Morning in Majorca

There is nothing as beautiful as the morning in Majorca. Of course, it helps if you are awake to see it. Mac was not. Mac was having one of those sleep-in mornings, one of those mornings that come after stay-out nights. For Mac there were many of these kinds of mornings because there were a lot of those kinds of nights. Mac liked to drink at a local bar, samba, even solo if no one would join him, and then dance his way into the little hours with one of the girls at a nearby brothel. He was popular with those girls. Not because he brought lots of money and wine on those staggering escapades. No. They loved him because he was fun. He certainly was fun last night. That is what he decided on his way home, even if the details were sketchy. In fact, how he made it back to his boat was a mystery.

He went out last evening without a care, ready for a night of fun. Then he heard that a letter arrived for him, and the news filled him with anxiety. He knew that this letter would change his life, in one direction or the other, forever. He thought he should go to visit Ernesto, the friend who was holding the correspondence, but it was late, and he wanted to be well-rested when he retrieved the life-changing dispatch. After all, the future is not something to jump into without preparation. He decided that abandoning pleasure at a reasonable hour and returning to his floating acropolis for sleep would be prudent.

But for Mac, prudence and pleasure were often at odds. He couldn't resist one more glass of wine, one more sensual serenade, one more casual caress. And the hours went by. Until, finally, shrouded in ecstasy and much later than anticipated, he bumbled his way to the dock and launched the dinghy for his boat. When he found his bed, he slept hard, lulled to the land of nod by the god of wine and the gentle sway of the waves of the bay that rocked his berth like a caring nanny would rock the cradle of a precious infant. And now, even though his future lay in the balance, he slept in besotted bliss while the day began in the most perfect place in the world.

From a boat in the bay, you can see the azure waters stretching before you and lapping at the golden beaches like the wet tongue of a persistent lover. In the harbor, rows of sturdy sailboats stand at attention as ready to serve as the bellmen at the best hotels. On the beach, carefully tended palm trees jut from the sand with majestic grace to offer relief to promenading seaside pedestrians. And behind the boulevard-bound beachfront, buildings collide, rising from clusters of tropical growth and sturdy oaks to elbow their way into the surrounding hills.

The calculated clutter is crowned at the east by the Cathedral Le Seu, also called The Cathedral of Santa Maria of Palma, which towers above all. This beacon of faith, with its Gothic architecture, buttresses into the fray and keeps vigilant guard, watching over the comings and goings of the taka-taka-rhythmed city. Even late at night, seafaring sinners can look to the spires and be reminded of their transgressions.

Beginning with dawn, the vista of this magical pandemonium is illuminated with increasing intensity until, at last, the sun peeks over the top of the eastern hills and streaks the day with the golden promise of adventure. It is an inspiring sight. If you are awake.

When Mac sauntered into consciousness, he thirsted for an antidote to his after-hours adventure. Under usual circumstances, he'd untie the dinghy and motor his way to a favorite onshore eatery for medicinal espresso, but this morning, late and foggy, he started coffee on the galley stove and waited for his eyes to focus. The propane tank was acting up again, and he gave it a kick. There was no time for more sleep or a fussy connection. This morning he wanted to be awake.

Tank tamed, and coffee brewed, he took his cup deckside and sat, absorbing the paradise before him. Majorca, Spain. An island of fiery flamencos, swarming sidewalks, hearty embraces and sensuous senoritas. This is a place where an American expatriate can live under the radar, moor his boat for free, and spend his time finding love. In Mac's case, the search for cash transactions of wine, women, and song was close enough. Mac learned that love is simplest when you pay outright.

Mac, dubbed by the Majorca locals, was Kevin by christening. He'd spent forty-five years of his laboring-life in the hard work of sales. He sold cogs, small plastic cogs, to manufacturers and saved every penny for his dream. His dream was to build a boat and sail around the world, stopping wherever he liked. That was his dream. And that's what he did. He sold, he saved, he stashed, he slaved. He built the boat, took his wife with him, because she would not stay behind, and together they sailed away much to the astonished disapproval of their then adult children.

They sailed everywhere: England, Spain, France, Italy, Florida and Maine. It was a long and adventure-filled journey. His wife thought they'd get bored and go home, and when they didn't, she said, "Enough." The discovery of the affair he was having with the new female crewmember served as the catalyst for her explosion and disembarkation. They separated. Still he sailed on from horizons, to ports, to vistas. They divorced, and on he went. Then his ex-wife became ill and died. But he did not mourn or moor. He sailed still.

He wasn't alone. He married the cozy shipmate, who became his second wife. But that didn't last. Ageist ambivalence caused her to turn to a handsome younger sailor. Kevin was enraged by this karmic betrayal. They divorced. And on he sailed. On and on, looking toward the next adventure, the next love, the next harbor.

That was how he got to the beautiful beehive-island of Majorca and made his way to the teaming city of Palma. That was how he arrived at this particular morning, in this particular place, by the belly of a sail and a thrill for life. Before this Eden, he was Kevin. Here he was Mac. Somehow that sounded like an appropriate handle for a crusty, if fun, self-made seafaring adventurer anchored in Majorca.

The coffee worked as an elixir, and now less shaky and more focused, he decided it was time to retrieve the letter that Ernesto was holding for him. The post wasn't delivered to a randomly moored vessel. The proprietor of his favorite local café allowed him to use that address. That was where the letter was delivered. That was where the letter was waiting, the letter that would fill him with limitless hope or send him into aggravated despair. Good or bad, curiosity would not let it go unopened. It was time to find out what fame and fortune the future held. He grabbed his favorite hat, snatched up his reading glasses, boarded the ship's dinghy, and headed for the shore, his favorite shore, the shore of Palma on the island of Majorca, Spain.

———

CHAPTER 2
Ernesto's

Ernesto's is a small old-fashioned bar and café situated on an alley-wide street just outside of Old Town in Palma. Palma with its population of half a million is besieged by millions of European vacationers during the summer months. The crush can be fun but assaulting. Ernesto's became an off-the-path sanctuary to Mac.

"Hola," Ernesto greeted as Mac entered the empty café. "How are you this morning?"

"Excellent, excellent, my friend. It was a rough start, but I am now ready for the day."

"Delores told me she heard you were out late last evening. And at another establishment," the bar owner jibed.

"One must spread the wealth," Mac said. "The women in the other bars deserve a chance."

"That is true," Ernesto said. "They cannot be forever deprived. But still, to dance all night?"

"Dancing is good for you," Mac said in his defense. "It is exercise for the spirit, the mind and the body. That is why I do it often. To stay fit."

"I will take it up," Ernesto retorted, "as soon as I do not have to work."

"Then, you and I will dance together all night and show the men of Majorca what it means to be alive," Mac said with comradery.

"Ha," Ernesto laughed. "You dance. I will sit, at last, with my feet up and watch."

Mac discovered the café on one of his first forays into the city. Avoiding the squares overrun with tourists, he sought a quiet side-street and came upon the establishment, the patio made welcoming by the shade of a large holm oak tree.

An outgoing personality, honed by years of salesmanship, gave the expatriate a gift for conversation. Mac once told the bar owner the secret of his success: "Keep talking until the customer buys something. Eventually, they do it just to shut you up." Ernesto, who also served as waiter, bartender, and sometimes cook shared his own secret: "Pour drinks and listen until they run out of energy or money." A talker and a listener need one another, and the two men became quick friends.

"Coffee or mail?" Ernesto asked.

"Let's put them both on the table and see which goes first." Mac, who prided himself on the illusion that he was of an even temperament, found he was as nervous now as he was last evening when he heard of the letter. He received mail at Ernesto's before. Letters of all sorts. Most recently, the letters held rejection. "Thank you for your enquiry, but we find . . ." Those started to arrive when he decided to pursue a career as a published author.

Mac was always interested in writing. As far back as he could remember, he was jotting down short stories, words for songs, ideas. His interest was diverted by marriage and family and life. But now that he was free from those burdens, he wanted to pursue that dream. Words are cogs, he thought. I sold cogs; I can sell words. In the last several years, he launched an attack on the world of literature by penning a series of light reading. No one who knew him could tell you for certain what motivated him. Some write for fame, others for money, and still others write for a reason they cannot put into words. Maybe they want to share a phrase or idea so that it will last for eternity. That may have been Mac's inspiration. Or perhaps he was bored. For whatever reason, he wrote story after story. And as he did, he sent his narratives to every publisher he could with the message, "You will love this." But weary readers of manuscripts sent their own messages, "Not for us."

Mac started with smarmy chick-centric tales. College girls off for a weekend in the big city. He thought readers would love young girls searching for their first big "O." He did. Mac had his own smarmy experiences for inspiration, and he believed the tales would cross over despite age and gender differences. But there were no takers. Publishers were not interested. After several stabs at virginal angst, he switched to detective fiction. In these stories, a self-proclaimed private investigator is hired by a suspicious client to find a killer or to uncover some secret or another. He loved writing them, spinning the plots to deceive and divert, but always with a victory for the hero who uncovered the truth in the end. He was sure these would be hugely successful. Editors, however, were as eager for these as they were for his girls-on-the-prowl efforts.

He received a considerable number of "No" letters but would not be deterred. He continued to write and rewrite. Change the characters, alter the verbs, amend the adjectives, and the story undergoes a metamorphosis. And while he crafted his work, he continued to hunt for an unsuspecting publishing source. He had been a salesman. Rejection rolled off of him. It is nothing to worry about, he'd often tell himself. There are a million opportunities. And if there were to be a million letters saying "No," let them arrive by the thousands. There would be one that said "Yes." It only took time. That is what he always thought, but that "Yes" was taking more time than he thought it would. And the numbers of "No" were taking a greater toll.

At first, the letters didn't bother him much. They were incentives. He rebounded from them with a lovely meal or a night of dancing. Then he noticed that he was having an extra drink along the way to dismiss an odd feeling. That extra drink turned to two or three. The alcohol filled him with a faith in his work he wasn't sure he really felt.

He kept all the "No" letters in a basket by the galley table on his boat. He planned to send each correspondent a copy of the review of his best-selling book when it exhibited itself. Letter by letter the basket filled. He would hire a secretary to complete the correspondence, he decided. Then the envelopes began to brim over.

One evening, about two weeks ago, he found there was almost no space at the table for a late-night snack. That was when he decided to count the letters. Twenty, forty — he had been busy. Sixty, seventy — it was a tribute to his diligence. Eighty, ninety — he was tenacious. When he tallied, there were ninety-nine letters, ninety-nine publishers who told him "No." Ninety-nine persons dismissed his work. Hmmm. One by one, he could soldier on, but with ninety-nine, he would have to confront the situation. After much thinking and several glasses of a nice wine he saved for many years, he decided. If he received one more letter of rejection, bringing the total to one hundred, he would stop. He would find something else to do with his time. He had no idea what it would be, but it would be. That is why he sat at Ernesto's feeling more uncertain than ever before. That is why this letter was so important to him. That is why he was reluctant to pick the envelope up off the table.

———————

———

CHAPTER 3
Find Him

Halfway across the world, in that small office in New Jersey, the phone rang. The man, seated at the desk, with his suit jacket hung on the back of the visitor's chair, checked the caller ID, and answered the phone.

"What have you got?" he asked with a flat voice that hid his curiosity.

"Not much," the voice said. "He was in London till seven years ago. St. Katherine's Harbor. But the dockmaster doesn't know where they sailed."

"Who's they?"

"He was married at the time."

"He remarried?" the New Jersey man asked with surprise.

"That's what the records show. Some Brit," said the caller.

"Did you locate the woman?"

"Found her name," the voice said. "Tried to call her family, but if they know anything, they are not telling."

"Where is she now?" asked the man in the office.

"Not sure. Maybe got remarried. Could have changed her name."

"Why would she hide?" the New Jersey man asked.

"It may not be deliberate."

"She must be some place. Find her."

"We're working on it," assured the voice.

"What about the boat? It's registered isn't it? Doesn't that make it easier?"

"Not every place keeps records," the hound said. "If it's in a legitimate harbor, there's a good chance it's on some book, but if it's anchored off a sand dune, it could sink, and no one would know."

"Look, time is running out." The man at the desk was insistent. "I need you to find him."

"It's expensive, you know," said the caller. "It'd cost less to let him disappear, if that's what he wants."

"I don't care what he wants. You work for me. I want him found." The man with the suitcoat hanging on the chair was definite.

"He must owe you big," the seeker said.

"Don't worry about that. Just send a bill. Keep me updated and find him. He has to be somewhere." He hung up, crossed to the window, and stared with annoyance into the darkening evening.

———————

———————

CHAPTER 4
The Letter

Ernesto placed the coffee on the table and positioned the letter next to it. Mac stared at the envelope. Ernesto waited, but the American did not move. After a minute, Mac picked up the envelope. He looked at it, held it to his ear and then to his nose. Resigned, he put it back on the table and sipped the coffee.

"Aren't you going to open it?" asked Ernesto.

"I know what it says," answered Mac. "I have dozens like it."

"You can't know that before you open it," insisted Ernesto.

"I can tell. It looks like 'No.' It sounds like 'No.' It smells like 'No.'" Mac spoke with certainty.

"How can you be sure?"

"I know," Mac said. "Throw it away."

"And suppose you are wrong. Then you will never know."

"I am not wrong," Mac said again. "I am not going to open it."

"Then, I will open it," said Ernesto, "the act of a friend." He took the letter and ran his finger under the flap. He scanned the contents. "It says 'No,'" Ernesto said in disappointment.

Mac knew what it said: "Unfortunately at this time, blah blah blah . . ." The would-be author tried to be gracious, but Ernesto could see the melancholy begin to descend, so he sat in the empty chair at the table and gave his best "They are crazy" speech. He peppered the tonic with phrases like "What do they know," "They could make millions," and "They have no intelligence."

Mac went from rejection to despair and then to anger in a matter of moments. When the pendulum of his emotions settled, he sided with Ernesto in outrage; the publishers lacked savvy, the readers lacked taste, and the clerks were stupid. The character he created, the amateur private investigator who always solved the mystery, had major syndication and movie possibilities even if the "idiots" could not see it. Not only was there a series of books to create, there were movies, and it was perfect for television. Yes, he was not the greatest writer since Tolstoy, but how many episodes of that Russian's work made it to the airwaves? No one wanted literature when they sat in their living rooms with popcorn and chips. They wanted crap. Cozy, convoluted, recognizable crap. He concluded by summarizing that yes, the novel was crap, but it was good crap.

"How long have I been coming to your place? Eight years? And every day, what do I do?" Mac asked.

"You talk to women," the proprietor answered.

"When I am not talking to women."

"You drink coffee," Ernesto said eager to be of help.

"When I am not having coffee?" the writer challenged.

"You dream of talking to women."

"That is true," Mac conceded, "but what else?" The proprietor looked perplexed. Mac continued. "I always have a book in my hand."

"It's true. You are often reading," Ernesto added with supportive gusto.

"But I am not reading," Mac corrected. "I am doing research."

"Ah ha," said Ernesto.

"All those big authors, all the ones on the bookstore racks, they have one thing in common," Mac summed up, "crap. They all write crap. Pages and pages of crap. They are all the same. Short chapters, lots of action, and a little sex."

"Sex is good," Ernesto agreed.

"Especially in chapters ten and twenty-two. I tell you, my friend, they all use the same formula. Crap. Crap. Crap. And yet they sell millions and millions of books. How come when I use the same recipe to write a book, the same chapter-by-chapter outline, no one wants to read it?"

"Because it's crap?" suggested Ernesto.

"No!" Mac declared. "It is because they are famous. When a famous author writes crap, it is best-selling crap. And when a nobody writes crap, it is no-selling crap." Mac rattled off a list of best-selling authors. "They all write crap, but they sell books because they are famous."

"So, be famous," Ernesto said.

"That is the trick, isn't it?" said Mac. "I am clever. I am fun. And I dance the samba with great flair, but none of those things make me famous." He took a long sip from the coffee allowing time for the paradox to settle. "To be famous, I need to be published. To be published, I need to be famous. It is a hopeless chase."

It was over. He would give up. How silly to think he could do it? His life was becoming an empty cavern. What could he expect from here? He was sinking into a dark sea just like his leaky boat, and the bilge was not working. What was left for him now? More nights of cavorting? Too much wine? Paying the national debt with his bordello bills? Until what? What happens to an old and unusable transplanted seafarer? What becomes of a man when he is too briny for a hard-working writer's life? Is he to sit and wait for the funeral pyre to transport his body into the ocean of the unknown? What a black day to be surrounded by rejection, to be veiled and undiscovered. What a dark moment to be him. "It is no use," he moaned to his friend. "It is no use being me."

"So, if it is no use being yourself," Ernesto said, "be someone else." And like a bolt, a light went on in Mac's mind. Someone else. He could be someone else.

———

CHAPTER 5
A New Plot

The greatest plans are often birthed in the darkest places. It is a matter of faith and genius. Mac spent the rest of the day plotting his meteoric rise to the best-seller list. Saved from the abyss by Ernesto's offhanded suggestion, Mac walked with renewed gusto through the streets of the city. From the grocery to the vegetable market, to the newspaper stand in a nearby hotel, Mac considered the future in the light of this new plan. If he couldn't convince, cajole, captivate, or charm the publishers into realizing that he was the greatest new writer to hit the presses, then he'd con them with a new tactic. He didn't need to be the "writer" himself. He could be the "representative" of the writer, the new author, an elusive and internationally sought-after phantom-superstar.

He thought of the fun of tricking everyone. How amazed they'd be when they found out the truth. All of those stories, every one of those best-sellers, were written by him. He delighted in imagining the faces of the unknown rejecters when they found out how wrong they had been in their easy dismissal of his mastery.

Thomas Chatterton had sold his stuff as the writings of a fifteenth century monk. James Macpherson claimed to have discovered a third-century epic by the bard Ossian, which in reality was a story Macpherson couldn't sell. Even the *New York Times* was not immune to literary masquerade. That prestigious paper published contrived volumes claiming to be Hitler's diaries that were written by a German forger. What a scandal that had been! And there was the famous hoax of the childhood memoir of a Cherokee Indian that became required reading in schools across America. "Little Tree" had turned out to be the imagination of a well-known political speechwriter, inked some fifty years after the fact and under an assumed name. Hell — Shakespeare. Who really wrote those plays?

Mac laughed outright with glee at the idea. People passing by were uncertain of the mental stability of the laughing man — older, not unkempt, but sea-worn — carrying a canvas bag of purchases and breaking into a hearty guffaw without any apparent cause. Indeed, Mac felt a little lunatic. He jigged a step every now and again, smiled at all things small and large, and sometimes bowed with a sweeping arm when he caught a fellow walker eyeing him with concern.

When his appetite alarmed the need for a repast, he hauled his cargo and his resurrected hope to a nearby eatery. Brilliance takes nutrition. He had known that for many years. So, when he was hungry and filled with inspiration, he ate. There at the table in the café, with a snack in one hand and a pencil in the other, he made notes in the book that he always carried for moments when genius enveloped him, or when he needed to jot down the phone number of a sexy young tourist beguiled by his patter.

One: Create a false identity. Two: Promote the shadow to the press. Stunts, sightings, successes, and sins. A series of publicity releases to pepper the internet with titillating tales and steamy mystery. Three: Sell the books. With enough intrigue, the publishers would overwhelm him with offers. First, he'd need a name. James,

Joe, Jack. He liked the sound of the name Jack. It packed a wallop. Jack what? He needed something strong, like a bull. Bovine? Jack Bovine. Maybe that was too pastoral. People might think of a cow instead of a bull. He needed a book of names. He and his wife had used one with their second child, their daughter. The other two were boys. Those names had been easier to choose. They had used the grandfathers' names. Names, names, names . . .

For a moment, his mind slipped away from Majorca, back before the sea, back before he was Ahab, back to his other life. He drifted to the days when he was the successful cog salesman with a wife everyone loved and those three, precious little-ones. Everyone would ask: "How are those three, precious little-ones? They are so precious. Those three children of yours are precious. So precious." People saw them as perfect and adorable children, but he knew what they were — parasites. First feeding off the mother, in the womb and at her breasts, and then sucking in everything they could. Sucking, eating, feeding — devouring all time, all hope, and all dreams for the next thirty years. And then, when you need them, when you need their love, they turn on you like the hungry animals they are. They eat everything, rob you of your sleep, and chain you to a life of providing until . . . until . . . He hadn't thought of his children in months. He hadn't thought of his long-ago home for years. He tried not to think of the past. What good is thinking of the past? The future is hard enough without the past. With the past, the future is impossible.

Back to the present, he thought, back to the task. Choose a hero. Choose a name. This was going to be harder than expected, he thought. There are millions of names. Millions of options. Each has its own connotation. Salvador. John. Euripides. Each creates a different emotional response. Oscar. Godfrey. Francois. Each has an appeal to different readers. How would he even begin? Maybe a phone book? Too local. He needed to give this some careful attention.

What's in a name? To a hormonal adolescent who is willing to drink a sleeping potion to escape parental supervision, not much; a rose is a rose. But in the writing game, a name was everything. Once a reader discovers a writer they like, and identify with the style and genre, readers will return to that author for other material. The author's name had to tell the reader what they can expect. That's why the moniker is important. He'd have to create a persona that would appeal to the buyers of his books.

So, who did he think the readers would be? They couldn't be too smart, or they'd be critical. The books were easy light-hearted fare. A way to pass the time. They wouldn't spark literary analysis or articles for academic journals. There was action, but not a lot of blood, war, or exploding weapons, so Mac couldn't picture a lot of men reading the books. These were grocery cart fillers, last-minute items for airline readers. They had some sex, but it wasn't heavy or hardcore, so he figured the readers would be women, women who longed for a bit of romance and a quick thrill between housekeeping chores, hair appointments, and family errands. What sort of a writer would those women read? A stalwart and hardy man brandishing sex appeal might be a bit intrusive. They'd want someone with whom they could identify. Someone cozy and kind but with a hint of mystery and sensuousness. Someone who did things the readers only dreamt of doing. And then he realized it — he needed a woman.

———————

CHAPTER 6
The Note

Back in the New Jersey office, the man with the coat hanging on the chair picked up the stack of mail his secretary had deposited on his desk. Mail. Why did people send mail? Why did his secretary put it on his desk? Why did he read it? He thumbed through the pieces: An invoice for some office supplies, a letter from a company wanting an appointment. It would be easier if they had emailed or phoned. Wouldn't that be better for everyone involved? Mail was old-fashioned. It was one more thing to be dealt with. One more thing to be stacked up somewhere. One more thing to be read, responded to, and filed or thrown away.

Solicitations, a catalogue for patio furniture — how had they gotten his address, he wondered? Here was a notice for a company that had not been at this address for more than a decade. He thought whether he should throw it in the trashcan or write, "Not at this address," and return it to the sender. He set it aside. A letter. So much work. Dear so-and-so and so-and-so. He wanted to throw the entire stack into the can. It would serve the antiquated senders right if they never got a reply. But as he turned the pieces over, one caught his eye.

It was an ordinary simple envelope, nothing expensive or luxurious, the sort of envelope you might buy at a cheap office supply store, but it had been addressed by hand. And there, in a curious and fragile attempt at printing, was his name. There was a return address, but no name, only a street number with a city and state from the Midwest. He didn't know anyone from that area of the country. Who could be writing? And what could they want?

He opened the envelope with the letter opener on his desk and his heart started pounding.

"Dear Michael,

I found your contact information on the internet. Are you the son of Kevin MacNeal originally from New Jersey? I am a friend of your father, and I am writing to know if you have heard from him in recent months? I keep in contact with him, but he hasn't answered my latest emails, and I am concerned. The last I heard, he was living on the boat off the shore of Majorca, Spain. Can you let me know if you have news?"

God bless the post office, Michael thought, and then he put down the letter, opened his desk drawer and took out the envelope he found that started this search. He opened the envelope and took out the photograph it held. Damn bastard, he thought, staring at the image. Damn disappearing bastard. Then, although his hands were shaking, and he wasn't sure the carefully crafted coffee would stay in his stomach, he picked up the phone.

———

CHAPTER 7
Finding a Girl

"I need a woman," Mac told Ernesto the next morning.

"You are a welcome client at many of the local bordellos," Ernesto pointed out.

"Not for that," Mac replied. "I have decided to become a woman."

Ernesto sputtered. "It may not always work anymore, but is that a reason to cut it off?"

"Not for me," Mac explained, "for the book. My writer will be a woman. I will find a woman to pretend to be the author." Mac launched into the explanation of his reasoning. Ernesto was used to Mac's long and detailed rationales. He listened to many of them, and it was sometimes difficult to follow the thread when patrons needed attention. At present, there were no customers, so the owner/waiter/bartender/cook/friend could offer his complete attention. When Mac concluded his closing argument, Ernesto nodded in agreement.

"My friend, you are a genius. That sounds as good as any possibility," he said. "Are there a lot of women writers?"

"That is the beauty of it. She will be rare. She will be esteemed. She will be unique."

"Ah, yes. Unique. That is good. Who will she be?"

"Well, I haven't got it all worked out. There are still some details to put in place." Mac shrugged. "That is the excitement of constructing a plan, we are discovering the pieces as we go."

Ernesto raised his glass of wine. "To discovering."

"To discovering," Mac echoed, and the men toasted.

Discovering can take time, or so Mac found out. Even if you know what you want, it doesn't always appear right away. Life has a way of dragging things on, of tying hope and patience to a tight tether. He'd been in enough tense situations to know how it went.

Finding a woman to be an accomplice was nothing compared to sailing a sixty-foot yacht across the sea. Sometimes, when he was more miles from land than a bird would fly, he'd come up against storm surges that threatened drowning his haven. He tried to be sensible in the charting of the course, staying to the coastline when weather was dicey, but even the most careful sailor is sure to battle the salt. Wind and waves, storms and rain, tested passion. It took a sailor with steadfast desire to satisfy and survive. Mac had persevered every time. He battened down the hatches and drank himself to sleep, hope and patience his only allies. He had survived those tempests. He did not give up then. He wouldn't give up now. He would find an ally for this plan. It only required patience and careful choosing.

He had considered his ex-wife, the second one, for the charade. She might play in for a cut. The first wife, now deceased, would have just as soon seen him drown. It wasn't always that way. In the beginning she seemed to be in for the long haul, but that changed.

His first wife had been a taskmaster. That is what he often said. He discovered that during the first year of their marriage. "Make more, do more, be more." That was her idea of loving motivation.

And in some way that was good for him. He liked fun, and in those early years, he may have pursued other ambitions rather than making money. But she would not allow it. Not that anyone who ever met her would think that. She was so charming and nice to everyone, everyone except him. With him she was exacting and cold. He'd endured her complaining Germanic nature up until the day the boat was finished. Then he said to her, "I'm going, and you can or not, that is up to you." It was his rebellion, but not his freedom. She decided to go with him. She wasn't letting him loop around the globe, spending the fortune without her. No way. And she loved him. She did. She did love him, despite it all . . . She was angry when she found out about things — past indiscretions, past mistakes, past . . . the past. It was always the past. How he hated to think of the past, but she was good at remembering. And she was good at reminding him that she remembered. And he was good at pretending that he didn't notice she was reminding him. Her reminding, his pretending; it was a relationship. Not a perfect one, but it was one they understood. Until . . . until . . .

He and his wife had sailed to Florida, intending to spend a month exploring coastal cities. They stayed for over two years. When the couple waved "toodle-oo" to the Sunshine State, they set course for the south of France. They planned to travel through the Straits of Gibraltar, but they heard it could be treacherous, so in Bordeaux, they hired a Parisian sailor to guide them. It was not a smooth journey. Seas were calm, but tempers were not. The successful American cog salesman and his wife clashed with the boisterous baguette, so when they docked at the island of Malta, they liberated the Frenchman from the shackles of employment. With thousands of miles of water still to cross, they'd need a new mate.

They did what they always did. They went to the bar at the local harbor and talked around.

One of the captains of another ship knew a guy, who knew a fella, who knew this young girl, who was hoping to find a crew job to take her back to England. She'd been adventuring by crewing, an alternative to the backpacking approach, and was ready to return home. A few days later they met. She was young and British with healthy curves and an eager disposition. They had hired her. And passion had fired.

It isn't hard to understand; you are thousands of miles from home on an adventure with no defining boundaries. One of you is middle-aged. And that is being kind, Mac thought. The other is young, voluptuous and ready for living. It wasn't a unique story. It was a cliché. But as all the great poets know, life is a cliché. And it's true. Mac had often said, "We live, we breathe, we work, we fall in love, we fall out of love, and we grow older. Some people die along the way, but for those of us who don't escape, we think life is a singular and unique experience because it is us doing it. We forget that everyone does it. Life, love, loss, and betrayal. One after another, each as the other, in one enormously humorous joke that keeps getting told." The memorable punch line of this big laugh was that it took a full two weeks before wife number one figured out what was going on between the captain and the mate.

By then Mac was hooked. He had been transfused with youth, and he wanted to be free. Ten miles from shore, the transgression was discovered. His wife made such a roar that the island shook. They returned to the dock, unloaded her things, and she flew off in a chartered jet to return to America. She called the children, cried, filed for divorce, talked ill of him to anyone who would listen, took half the money, and then got cancer and died in a blazing light of sympathy as the martyr to a horrible self-centered husband.

The British miss was elevated to position of first mate, and after the seas had calmed, became wife number two. Not bad for a lassie from a family of pub owners in a one-street village in England. It had lasted for several years, but international water-travel is not for everyone. Not forever. An eternity of shifting horizons can immobilize a sense of stability, and some people, this woman in particular, wanted terra firma. They separated and then divorced when she met a less than attractive accountant with a steady job and a small parcel of family land.

Still they had remained "talking" friends, and he thought of her now as he foraged his mind for an accomplice in his plan. One of the downsides to continual relocation is a shortage of reliable friends. There were one or two here and one or two there. Reliability grows with roots, and constantly sailing away creates impermanence in love and friendship. There were a lot of ports, but not a lot of friends he could count on.

But his second wife, she could do it. She could impersonate the author. She had the right looks — British and comfy with a hint of deadly exuberance in her eyes. People would believe her. She could lie like any man in a fleet. And she might enjoy being the center of attention, having her photograph snapped at gala openings and saucy nightclubs. They shared enough secrets and knew enough dirt on one another that they might partner well for such a plan. But in the end, he didn't trust her. When push came to shove, she had given him up for a garden. How could he be certain that she wouldn't sell him out for a few thousand to help with the house? And she wanted children. Women who want children change when they give birth.

The bonds of marriage are often forgotten when stronger umbilical ties come into play. He ruled her out. No, if there was to be a woman who served as his invented author, it would not be her. He'd need to find someone who would buy in on her own.

He'd keep his eyes alert now, watching, looking for the perfect ally. And when he found her, he'd launch his successful assault on the book printers of the world.

———————

CHAPTER 8
The Investigator

It was about three weeks after the birth of Mac's plan when the stranger came into Ernesto's café. Ernesto was counting supplies, preparing to place an order for the following weekend, when the man walked in. He had a small bag over his shoulder with what appeared to be an elaborate camera lens showing from the top. "Good morning," Ernesto had said.

"Good morning," the man replied.

"Would you care for something to drink? We have an excellent vintage on hand, or I could make you a coffee. Maybe something to eat?"

"A glass of wine, thank you," said the man.

Ernesto got the glass, and the man sat at the bar. This intrigued Ernesto for almost no visitor to the café sat at the bar in the morning. They always preferred the picturesque patio or the view from the table by the window, not the darkness at the back of the café. Still it is no offense to be unusual, Ernesto thought.

Ernesto served the man a glass and stood there, continuing with his task. "Are you enjoying your holiday?" he asked.

"I am not on holiday, though it is beautiful here."

"Your camera," Ernesto indicated. "So many people on holiday come with their cameras."

"Ah, yes. I almost always carry mine with me," said the man, "for work and pleasure."

"You are a photographer?" Ernesto asked.

"Sometimes," the sometime-photographer said. "I am here, looking for someone, a man."

"Palma is friendly," Ernesto said. "And we do not judge. There is a place here for everyone."

"Not in that way," said the man. "I am trying to find a man who has disappeared."

"You are a detective?"

"An investigator. A representative, if you will."

"Someone in Palma?" Ernesto inquired.

"We are not certain. Only that he may be in Majorca."

"There are a lot of people on this island. Right now, it is the tourist season."

"This man might live here. On a boat," the investigator insinuated.

"There are a lot of boats," Ernesto said, "lots of harbors and places to moor."

"There are many here in Palma. I have been to dozens of them," the man said.

"Yes. We are the capital city, and we have a beautiful bay. It is popular."

"I can see," the investigator said.

"What did he do?" Ernesto asked, "The man you are hoping to find? Is he a criminal?"

"I am not here in an official capacity. I am trying to locate him for his family. They are eager to find him. Do you get a lot of strangers in your café?"

"Some, I suppose," Ernesto returned. "I have never seen you before."

"It's a nice café. Quiet and out of the way," the man said. "It's a place I might like if I lived here on a boat."

"Who is this man?" Ernesto asked.

"His name is Kevin."

"Kevin. Kevin. I do not think I remember anyone named Kevin," Ernesto tossed.

"MacNeal. Kevin MacNeal," the hired man clarified.

"No one I know."

The representative nodded his head but continued. "He may call himself by another name. He is older. In his seventies. About six feet tall. Probably gray hair. He is fond of women, I understand."

"Many men are," Ernesto replied. "I have an interest in them myself. It is an interest my wife does not appreciate."

"You are lucky to have a practical wife."

"I remind myself of my fortune every day." Ernesto moved a rack of glasses to the under-bar shelf.

"This man is American. He is outgoing, I understand. He used to be a salesman."

Ernesto knew he was being watched. He tried not to let any hint of possibility show, but bit by bit he began to wonder.

The investigator reached into his bag and took out an envelope. From it, he took a photograph. "Here is a photo. Have you seen this man before?"

Ernesto took the photograph and studied it. It was taken many years ago. A family event it seemed, still there was no mistaking. The man in the photograph was Mac. "Hmm." Ernesto said, "No one comes to mind. I see so many people in a season. But I don't think so."

"Well, thank you," said the man replacing the photograph in his bag. "I appreciate your taking the time." And then he stood, placed money on the bar, and pulled the bag once more onto his shoulder.

"I'm sorry I couldn't be of more help. Good luck," Ernesto offered.

The man nodded, heading back into the late morning sun. Ernesto watched as the "representative" walked down the street. There was something in the investigator's step that made Ernesto certain the man did not believe him.

———

————

CHAPTER 9
The Woman with the Princess Diana Haircut

The woman with the dark-blonde hair and the new Princess Diana style cut sat at her desk in her London office, reviewing the changes she'd made to the insurance documents she was working on. Liability and loss legalese can be draining, and she was eager to finish this set of contracts, have them signed by the boss, and messenger the lot to the client. She enjoyed her job, she did, and it paid her well enough to provide a comfortable living, but in the past months she had felt more and more unfulfilled by the work. Insurance is an odd business. It is like throwing dice. The wager is that the premiums the clients pay will outweigh any settlement paid if tragic circumstances fall on the clients' businesses. To her, it seemed odd to be in a business that depended on people who were part statistical experts and part fortune-tellers. She'd started with the company many years ago as a secretary and had advanced through time to the position of agent's assistant, which was much like a secretary but with an office. It was fine; it was steady, and the company had been lucky and profitable through the years. Still, it wasn't much fun to wait for a ship to sink or a factory to explode, and the tedium of editing insurance policies and shuffling paper offered little relief to a thirty-something woman with no definite romantic prospects.

Tenure at the job did come with a few advantages. One of them was paid holiday time. She had three weeks a year, and when the strain of a dull future became too overwhelming, she could look forward to time away. Finishing this contract would be her last task before a much-needed vacation. That was why she altered her hair style. She wanted something to launch her trip, and a new look always helped. The cut was out of fashion, she knew, but she didn't care; she liked it. It would be easy to care for, and a classic is a classic.

After she finished the alterations in the papers, she printed them, collected the necessary label, envelope, and messenger request forms and took the bundle to her boss for signature. "Here are the Ludwig Line policies," she said.

"Yes. Thanks. Put them in the stack," her boss replied without looking up. Her boss was a small gray man with a finicky way of moving. He was exacting when he adjusted his spectacles. He was precise when he used his pen. He was meticulous when he struck through clauses. He worked with efficiency, that was certain, but there was no joy. For the past months, the lady with the Princess Diana hair style had watched, looking for some sense that her boss enjoyed being fastidious. But she had seen none. He worked, and he was effective like an automated machine, she thought, but there was no excitement. Sometimes, she wondered if he ever smiled. If he ever laughed. He never spoke of his personal life, and even after many years, the agent's assistant knew almost nothing of this man. In recent months, she had noticed that she was becoming more like her boss than she felt comfortable with.

"If you have a moment to sign them," the agent's assistant said, "I'll have them delivered to the client."

"What? Oh, I see. Yes. You're on holiday next week, aren't you? I'd almost forgotten. Done, dusted, and on the shelf, that's the strategy?" her boss asked.

"Yes," she answered, "and I did promise the client."

"Wouldn't want to disappoint. Let's have a look, shall we?" Her boss set his work aside, took the papers she handed him, and began peering through them. "Yes. Fine. Good hefty premiums."

"The line has strong resources, and they are getting quality coverage," she said.

"Well done, Elizabeth. You keep up this level of work, and you'll be ready for management soon," her boss said.

Soon, Elizabeth thought. She had been with the company for over fifteen years. How old would she be when soon arrived?

"Here you go," her boss said, signing the documents. "If you'll witness here." He pointed to the signature page. Elizabeth added her mark on the appropriate line, Elizabeth Schoenhauer. "So, a little rest and relaxation, eh?" the executive asked. "Are you staying in the city?"

"No," said Elizabeth. "I'm heading to sun and warmth."

"Not Ibiza, I hope," he said with trepidation. "That place, I hear, is an island of debauchery." The island had that reputation. The younger set loved the idea of sunny beaches, as many drinks as you could consume without pitching them up, and as much sex as the conscious hours allowed. But Elizabeth had never been one of the wild crowd. The idea of carefree abandon always seemed to her an uncapturable experience. She was the sort of person who would spend more time worried that she was missing the thrill, or worse, that she hadn't missed it at all. Either way there was no carefree abandonment for her. She wondered what it would be like to throw caution to the wind and live with daring.

"No. I am heading to someplace a little saner. I am going to Palma, Majorca," she told him.

"Be sure to see the cathedral," the executive said without looking up, "and wear a nice floppy hat. The sun can be strong."

She made a copy of the document and went back to her office. She put the agreement into a labelled envelope and completed the messenger slip, placing the package in the outgoing-mail tray. Then she collected her personal things. As she was leaving her office, she remembered and opened her desk drawer, taking the travel brochure with her. She hoped Palma was as beautiful as the photos in the advertisement. She also hoped she found something exciting there. She needed something exciting. Maybe she would throw caution to the wind and purchase a large floppy hat.

CHAPTER 10
A New Day

There is nothing as beautiful as the morning in Majorca. Mac thought that every time he saw the dawn. On days when he was looking forward to something extraordinary, he found the experience even more invigorating. A new beginning, that was the dawn. Forget the night before. Forget the past. The thing that matters is now and what is coming. What came before was only a prelude to a wonderful future.

He sat on the deck, taking his energizing morning coffee and watching the sky. Another magnificent day. This is what he had always imagined paradise would be. A perfect day, a perfect plan, and a perfect cup of coffee. It was a reason to cheer. He considered raising the sail and taking the vessel for a celebratory circle around the bay, but he remembered the winch had jammed, and he couldn't hoist the sail until it was repaired. Damn boat takes upkeep. It used to be a pleasure, now it was a pain. A pain in his hand, a pain in his shoulder, a pain in his ass. He would put the winch on his ever-growing list of things to take care of in the future. That was for tomorrow. For now, he turned his attention to the task at hand, finding a cohort. It had been three weeks since the plan had been laid, and he still had not found a suitable accomplice. Well, maybe today would be the day. Why not today? It was a beautiful day, and on a beautiful day, all things were possible.

He had arranged a tarp between the mast, which had sprouted a new patch of splinters, and the cabin, whose window needed a new waterproof seal, creating a makeshift awning for shade as the sun rose to a heated zenith. Feeling a bit warm, he moved into the covered area and laid his head back against the cabin, breathing in the crisp salty air. The clang of his cup falling to the deck startled him. He had nodded off. Napping so early and with so much to do; that was not like him. He took his bearing, shook off the haze and headed below to check his computer in case there was an inquiry about his novel. Nothing. That will soon change, he thought, and then he gathered the necessities to assemble his "to-the-shore" bag.

Once on land, as was his habit, he went to Ernesto's to catch up with his Palma friend. When he arrived, he was surprised to find the café closed. That is unusual, Mac thought, one of the children must be ill. There were few things that would keep the bar owner from business. Ernesto's wife would not allow a shuttered day unless there was ample need. Mac would check back later and make sure all was well.

Continuing with his errands, Mac stopped at the bank to send a message to the only person from the past with whom he still communicated. Her name was Sally. He thought of her as his secretary, but she handled all of his business affairs for more than forty years. He earned her steadfast devotion with respect, loyalty, and a considerable retirement fund. He treated her better than either of his wives, and she returned his favor with diligence, silence, and an impenetrable presence. The best part of the arrangement was that no one knew of her. Together they managed to remain undiscovered, even through a nasty divorce. It took a lot of effort, but coded correspondence to an unknown wire and untraceable calls from pay phone boxes made it possible.

It was true, Mac was a successful salesman, but he parlayed his earnings by making several investments that may not have been entirely on the up and up. He set up a shell company to make sure the money could not be traced. And if he sensed that someone was looking, he did what he did with his boat and moved.

Mac disappeared so many years ago, that he was pretty certain no one could follow the cash. Uncle Sam is a stickler when it comes to tithing, but it irritated Mac to pay hard-earned money for nothing. And as far as he knew, the American government did little for him and did not need the money. He kept his secretary, Sally, out of the loop so she would not be at risk. Maybe his caution was unnecessary, but to date, discretion paid dividends, and he preferred to keep it that way.

After Mac sent disbursement instructions from the bank, he made several other stops completing the list of errands. Business done, he headed toward the seafront promenade, hoping to find his favorite bench unoccupied. The perch he preferred was in a secluded area facing the beach, where he could watch the comers and goers and have a good, uninterrupted think. He didn't make it that far. As soon as he turned to the promenade, he saw her.

————

CHAPTER 11
Tracking Mac

After his meeting with Ernesto, the investigator waited out of sight. It only took a few moments. The barkeep emerged with a light jacket, locked the door, and walked off down the street. Bad for business, thought the man with the camera, and adjusting the lens, took a few photographs of the departing café owner. Ernesto moved off in the direction of the port, and the man followed.

They walked that way, in covert tandem simpatico, till the Spaniard went into a small shop near the harbormaster's office. The operative walked past the shop window but couldn't get a clear view of what was conspiring inside. In a few moments, Ernesto left the office. The investigator decided to wait it out and see what, if anything, happened. A little later, a speedboat launched with hurried purpose from a nearby waterway, cutting a slice on the bay and heading toward the westward part of the harbor. Not as fast as a cell phone, thought the man, but much more fun to watch. He assumed the boat was dispatched with news to the replanted Mr. MacNeal.

When he was certain of the direction in which the boat was headed, and it had disappeared into the spray, the investigator visited some of the neighboring businesses. In each he presented the photograph and asked, in badly managed Spanish, if anyone recognized the subject. His inquiries were met with reluctance. The locals could smell a bad fish out of water, and a foreigner asking questions, even in a place like Majorca, made them suspicious. Most followed the adage, "Silence is golden," preferring to say they did not recognize the person in the photograph, or that they did not understand what was being asked. But for a few, discreetly presented currency served as an effective interpreter. He found the confirmation he sought.

The man in the photograph was indeed living in Palma. He owned a small boat harbored off the dock of a nearby hotel. The seafarer, according to those who would talk, was anchored here for at least seven years. He came to town often, buying provisions and raising a late-night ruckus at local taverns. His drunken antics drew more attention than his history. Most spoke with generosity. The drifter was, at least in some small way, a part of the community. They did not know much about him, not before his ship sailed into the harbor and anchored. They knew he was an American, lived on the boat, and went by the name of Mac.

He asked a few more questions about docking for daily shopping and was pointed in the general direction of the public-accessible slips. He went that way to watch and wait, intending to be as patient as necessary. But it did not take long. Within thirty minutes, the sought-after sailor tied his vessel to the dock and started up the ramp toward the city.

Keeping his head down, with a hat to block the sun from his face, the tracker followed at a safe distance. He blended into groups of sightseeing visitors, pretending to examine displayed merchandise and taking photographs as they moved.

He followed Mac to the shuttered café and noted the look of surprise on the self-proclaimed seaman's face. He shadowed Mac to the bank, observing from across the street. The agent did not follow the subject into the establishment. Even though he was curious about the business being conducted, he thought it best to keep an invisible distance. When Mac left the financial institution, the snooper tailed him from errand to errand, catching glimpses of the target in his viewfinder. Then the man with the camera watched with curious interest as the man he was following spotted the dark-blonde woman, sitting on a bench on the promenade, and moved toward her.

———

———

CHAPTER 12
Elizabeth

She was sitting on his favorite bench along the boardwalk, and he spotted her in an instant. Her short cut dark-blonde hair framed two exuberant eyes and a longish nose that seemed designed to draw attention to her thin, gentle, and inviting lips. She had a bemused expression on her features as if what she saw made her smile. She emitted a no-nonsense aura, an intriguing contrast to the pleasure that seemed to wink in her eyes.

She sat with confidence and ease at the same time, and Mac got the impression that she could handle any situation with style. He liked grace in women, true grace, not the affected pretense he saw in those hoping to make an impression, or the casual sloth of those who did not care about their lower-class breeding. A woman who brought grace into the world made life more beautiful just by being present. Mac appreciated that.

Mac, who felt the direct approach disarmed potential defense, walked to the bench and spoke. "How would you like to make a lot of money?"

The girl, surprised and uncertain of this assault, looked up at him, and then back to the water. "You have the wrong person. I am here on holiday."

"I knew you were a visitor. I could tell right away. You're English," Mac exclaimed.

"And you must be American," the woman said.

"Why do you think so?" Mac asked.

"You have that horrible accent," she said, "and are presumptive in the way I have only experienced with people from your country. If you were Latin, you would have started by telling me I was the most beautiful creature you have ever seen, more beautiful than the sights of this panorama. If you were German, you would have said something like 'I am the man to be the father of your children.' But to make a business proposition in the first instant — that takes an American."

"I'm Mac," Mac extended his hand.

"And I am not interested," the girl said and stood as if to leave.

"Don't go." He reached out a hand. "Not just yet. Let me talk with you."

"I told you I am not a working girl. I am not a hooker," she flared.

"I didn't mean it that way. I am not looking for a prostitute. If I was, I'd go to one of the brothels in the area. I am a preferred customer at several of them. This is something else. A legitimate business proposition. Sit with me and let me tell you about it, and if you are not beguiled and intrigued, as I believe you will be, I can buy you lunch, say goodbye, and wish you a wonderful holiday."

She was on holiday; that was true, although she didn't like that he so easily identified her as a visitor. Tourists fall into two categories: Those who are vacationing, and those who think no one can tell they are vacationing. The English woman was one of the second group. With no camera at her hand, and a simple and tasteful casual outfit, she did not think she looked like a person on an adventure. The man possessed the sharper eye. The fact, as she remembered, was that she had come to Majorca with the expressed hope of some sort of adventure.

She recalled that her life in London was too routine, and she needed this carefree getaway to re-energize her soul. The photos of the island in the travel brochures conjured cozy restaurants, beautiful vistas, nightlife and romance. She read articles by visitors, all thrilled with their experience. And the flights were a reasonable price. She made her plans and came. To see, to find, to have something unexpected, something new. A legitimate business proposition wasn't the vacation memory she hoped for. Still, there would be nothing to remember if she turned from every possibility.

"All right," she agreed. "We'll sit here." She sat back down, Mac taking the other end of the bench. "I'm Elizabeth," she said.

"It is a wonderful name. Elizabeth," Mac said it, trying out the sound. "Consecrated to God."

"I prefer the meaning 'satisfaction.'"

"I love that," Mac declared. "Satisfaction is contentment, pleasure and gratification. It shows in your eyes. It is a perfect name."

"What sort of name is Mac?" she asked.

"It's Gaelic," Mac told her. "There is Scottish heritage someplace in the family line. I have handsome calves and look masterly in a kilt."

"Mac is also a common term for guy, or fellow, isn't it? People use it when they don't know a man's name and don't care to find it out. Is it your birth name?"

"No. But it is what people call me since I moved here."

"You live in Palma?" Elizabeth asked.

"Well, sort of. I have a yacht, over there." He pointed toward the mooring.

Elizabeth looked in the direction he pointed. "That big white one is yours?

"No, that little one, out beyond. The one with character," Mac said.

She peered. "Oh," she said with kindness. "It's a bit worn. But it looks charming."

"Age has a beauty all its own," Mac said. "It's not as shiny as something new, but there is a sturdiness and comfort that come with survival."

"I can see that," Elizabeth agreed. And indeed, she could. It showed in Mac as well as the boat. The lines around his eyes, the creases in his forehead and the sag in his neck gave warmth to a weathered face that spoke tales. Whoever he was, Elizabeth knew he had seen much. Did the crow's feet come from seeing too many wonders? Were the laugh lines leftovers from luxurious liveliness? The furrows in his brow might be the consolidated badge of careful consideration or intense apprehension. As she looked at him closely, she found herself interested in knowing more. "I think I am a bit peckish," she said. "Let's go to one of the nearby cafeterias for a snack, and you can tell me about this legitimate business proposition." Mac was quite happy with himself. He still had the gift. Together they stood and walked off in the direction of the shopping district.

Down the promenade, the investigator watched with dismay. The man must have picked up the dark-blonde woman. They were walking off. She didn't look like a hooker. He pegged her for a tourist. But they were talking, almost flirting it seemed, and now they were leaving together. The man was at least two generations beyond her. He dressed in rumpled old clothing. His boat needed maintenance, and he habituated the least expensive bar. Still, he acted as if he had no worries. And he was able to pick-up dark-blonde women at the beach side. He must have money. That was probably why the family hired him to find the man. Money. It is almost always about the money, he thought. Then he took his cell phone from his pocket and dialed to report.

———

CHAPTER 13
Word is Sent

Ernesto walked as quickly as possible back to the café. He wanted to return to work before anyone discovered his absence. His wife would be angry if she knew he closed the business for even a minute. More than once, she said that a customer who comes to a business when it is closed, does not return. She was right, but in this instance, an exception was needed. He felt it was important to get word to his friend. The friend went to a small-boat rental place at the harbor. The business was owned by one of his cousins who had a son, Enrico, who could be hired to run tourists to beaches or nesting cruise ships. The cousin met Mac at a family celebration, and he was happy to send a message. Some things are more important than a euro, thought Ernesto, if not to his wife, at least to him.

Ernesto did not know what the investigator wanted, but it was suspicious for anyone to ask. The natives liked to gossip, but to have a stranger inquire about anyone who lived here was an alarm. The bar owner was eager to be certain that Mac knew someone was asking about him. When he got back to the café and saw no sign that his truancy was noticed, he busied himself restocking the bar but kept glancing at the people passing by. He was on the lookout for Mac, of course, and his wife, in case, but also for the man who was not a tourist.

Lunch patrons began to arrive, but Mac still did not appear. Ernesto was busy catering to the customers' needs, which almost distracted him from worrying about his friend but not completely. What sort of trouble could it be, he wondered in between orders. The investigator said he was searching on behalf of the family. That was odd because Ernesto couldn't remember Mac talking about them. He knew Mac was married twice, one wife passing from an illness, the other living with a new husband in England, and Ernesto thought Mac fathered children, but none of the details were clear to him. He'd seen no photos. He knew nothing of their conversations. He didn't even recall knowing Mac's childrens' names. It was strange, he thought, parents usually speak endlessly of their offspring, but if someone did not, who was he to wonder why. And Ernesto didn't. Never. Not until that morning. Now, he was curious.

Families can be a breeding ground for agitation. Ernesto knew that from his own flock. Some people speak often of that friction, happy to complain of the anxiety or grief inflicted by relations. Others preferred to refrain from conversing about it all together. Now Ernesto found himself wondering what disquiet exiled the subject of family from Mac's conversation. He didn't want to intrude, but he hoped Mac knew that if he needed an ear, he'd be happy to lend his. And he vowed, at least to himself, that he would offer little to no advice, only sensitive support.

It was after one o'clock when Mac came in, grinning from ear to ear. "I found her," he told Ernesto. "I found my writer. Her name is Elizabeth. We will call her Elizabeth Kensington. That will be her name. Isn't that a wonderful name? The perfect name." Mac proceeded to outline the meeting, his impressions of Elizabeth, and the details of the arrangement they made at lunch. "She is perfect," Mac told him. "The publishers will eat her up."

"Did Enrico find you?" Ernesto asked when Mac paused for a breath.

"No. Was he trying to?"

"Yes. I sent him to your boat with a message," Ernesto said.

"I didn't see him," Mac reported. "What was the message?"

"There has been a man here, asking about you."

"If I were younger, I'd suspect it was an angry husband, but since my love life is restricted to cash, I don't think that is the case."

"The man said he was an investigator, an agent of some kind."

"He must be looking for someone else," Mac said.

"He has a photograph of you," Ernesto disclosed.

"A photograph of me?" Mac was astonished. "How is that possible?"

"It looked as if it was taken some years ago," Ernesto went on. "He said he was looking for you on behalf of your family."

"Then I know he is confused. I do not have a family," Mac said with force.

"It is what he said," Ernesto assured.

"My family is dead."

"You told me you were married twice," Ernesto said.

"On this day, when I have found the perfect woman for my hopes, do you need to remind me of my younger failures?"

"Do you have children?" Ernesto asked.

"None I claim," Mac said.

"But did you have children with either of your wives?" Ernesto pressed.

"Does it matter?"

"Not to me," Ernesto said with ease. "Only, if you did, the man may have gotten the photo from them."

"A photograph? What photograph? I haven't told anyone where I am. I sent one postcard to a friend, one, but that friend doesn't know my family. There were letters to the publishers, but I used a pseudonym. How could anyone find me here? My children. Leave it to them to try and make a mess of my happiness again. Mac relented, sat at the bar, and sighed. "Yes, I have children, three of them. Two sons and a daughter."

Ernesto let a quiet moment pass. "I don't think you ever mentioned them."

"We aren't close," Mac told his friend. "We aren't in contact." They stole enough of my time when I was younger; I won't give more to them now, Mac thought.

"I see. Then why are they looking for you?" Ernesto asked.
"Money, I bet." Mac shrugged it off. "It was always money with them." It was, he reminded himself. When they were younger there was always the latest trinket, the newest fad, updated technology, or trendier clothes to add to the piles stuffed in their closets. And then when they got older and simple was no longer enough, it was a new car, a motor scooter, or a trip to some expensive location. The more costly, the more it was desired. With the children, it was always money. That's what he remembered. And disagreement. Quarrelling, clashing, conflict. His mind drifted off to an unhappy time, a time when pressure outweighed pleasure, and life was strife.

Ernesto must have sensed something because he asked, "Did you do something wrong?"

"No," Mac said with force. "No, I did nothing. No. There was a misunderstanding, that is all. There was screaming and accusations. But they were wrong. I am not a bad person." Mac stopped.

Ernesto knew he had touched a nerve. If you say you are not in pain, but are bothered by the doctor's probe, then you are wise to consider a complete examination. "Is it something you want to talk about? You know I will listen without judging," Ernesto assured Mac.

Mostly what Mac wanted was to let the subject pass. He began in a new direction. "We are not even sure who this man is. We don't know what he wants or how he came to your café. I don't think he was looking for me. I have an ordinary face. It may have been anyone in that photo. Your eyes, you know they are not good. And the light here, well, it is dark, and can make it difficult to see clearly. And why would anyone be looking for me? I have my passport. I have my boat papers. There is no point in worrying. You cannot stop someone from looking, even if they are searching for the wrong person."

Ernesto waited a moment before asking, "Is your given name Kevin, Kevin MacNeal?" Mac's face went white and Ernesto knew it was true. The investigator was searching for his friend.

"I am Mac," Mac said. "Kevin MacNeal died a long time ago. Somewhere off the coast of France. Let us not mourn for him. He lived a life and is free. If there is a man searching for him, then he is looking for a ghost," Mac said. "For now, let us assume this is an error of identification, and let's see how things develop. It may be nothing. There's no reason to worry about what we do not know, all right?"

"All right," Ernesto agreed.

"And let's keep this between us, my friend. I invited Elizabeth to come here tonight. I want you to meet her. I want to see what you think. I believe she is perfect, and I don't want to scare her with stories of ghosts."

———

CHAPTER 14
Instructions

"Majorca? You saw him?" Michael asked.

"I am pretty certain it is him," the investigator assessed. "I kept a distance but got some decent pictures."

"Can you send me the photos? I want to see. If it is him, I want to know."

"I'm transferring them now," the hunter said. "It shouldn't take more than a few minutes."

"How does he look?" Michael asked. Is he old, he thought. Has he gone bald? After all these years, will he even be recognizable?

"You will see soon enough," the agent proclaimed.

The computer chimed, announcing a delivery to Michael's email-box and he opened the incoming message. He stared at the screen profoundly surprised, relieved, angry, frightened, and shaken.

"Is that him?" the man asked.

"Yes," Michael confirmed. "That is him."

The man on the ground in Majorca waited a moment and then continued. "Do you have instructions? How would you like me to proceed?" Michael thought of a million things: Slap him, hug him, tie him up and put him in a trunk, then sink it in one of the damn seas he sailed. But he kept those ideas to himself.

Michael considered the possibility of this moment. What if the investigator was successful in finding his father? What would Michael do? He had a plan, but he didn't know for certain if he would put it into action. Not until this moment. "I'm coming over," Michael decided. "It will take a couple of days to make the arrangements."

Hmm, the investigator thought, he is coming in person. This must be important. "Do you want me to approach him?" the spy asked.

"No. Don't tip our hand," Michael instructed. "Just watch him. Keep an eye on him. He has a way of disappearing."

"No problem. Now that we know where he is, it may not be easy to disappear."

You don't know him, Michael thought. He is an artist.

———

CHAPTER 15
A Moonlight Meeting

The day passed in a mix of carefree jauntiness and uneasy concern. Mac was excited about the prospect of the evening and his meeting with Elizabeth, but he was also wary of what Ernesto reported. The idea that any one of his family even considered sending someone to find him confused and confounded him. Somewhere deep inside, a fear always lived that he'd be faced with the past once more. Kindness is never remembered, but ill will haunts forever. And whether or not there was any merit to the report that he was being sought after, he was right; there is no point in worrying about it. It is like the rain; it will come, or it won't, and there is no way to stop it. He had an engagement with a lovely lady for the evening and a plan for the future. On he would sail into the night with the enchanting Elizabeth and her Princess Diana style haircut.

For the occasion, Mac put on his best pair of casual khaki slacks, a solid color T-shirt and his favorite tropical-print short-sleeve shirt. He liked the slacks because they made it look as though he still carried an ass. Asses are funny; with age you may become one and lose one at the same time. It seemed a little unfair; at the time of your life when your spine can use the cushion, it has disappeared. That is the price one pays for living. Sagging and withering are all a part of the eternal mystery.

He and Elizabeth arranged to meet at the bench of their first encounter and then walk together to Ernesto's. It was a sentimental idea, but Mac liked consistency. He always found luck in order, and he was excited to find it now in the midst of this new complication. Mac couldn't wait to introduce Ernesto to his new discovery. This would be the launch of his plan. The first official outing. All hail Elizabeth Kensington. That afternoon, he went to a local electronics store and bought a small digital camera so he could capture the evening's moments for the press campaign — "Novelist Cavorts at Majorca Club," or "Palma Hotspot Celebrates Writer." Those would be nice posts to accompany the photos, he thought, a great way to begin.

When Mac headed out, it was a perfect summer night. A slight breeze, an even temperature and blazing stars in the sky. There was something about living in the harbor and crossing the water to the dock that filled him with a mystical sense of adventure. He was the explorer, and the night was unchartered territory. Smooth waters or rocking tides, the journey was always exciting and blanketed him with expectation. He made his way ashore, secured the dinghy and then walked to the appointed place on the promenade. He sat on his favorite bench, waiting for the fascinating young woman and the start of his destiny.

The new toast of the literary world arrived promptly and was dressed for success. She wore a light summer shift flared from the waist, with a gold belt and matching bracelets on her wrist. Her seductive peek-a-boo leather sandals matched the small clutch in her hand. It was just the sort of impish effect Mac pictured for a best-selling author. She wore a scarf around her shoulders in anticipation of a cool night, and on her head was the perfect hat. A floppy-brimmed beige number that set off her holiday tan and her dark-blonde Princess Diana-like hair. She was a vision in every way that Mac hoped. This was the personification of his mythical author. This was radiance. This was style. This was Elizabeth Kensington.

She paused for effect, striking a pose with her hat that was half-way between mysterious and provocative, and Mac embraced her in delight. "You look wonderful," he said. "Perfect." And they took off toward the old part of the city, toward Ernesto's, where wine and music were waiting.

That morning at lunch, Mac had spelled out the plan to Elizabeth. She would play the part of his newly discovered author. He would arrange the media relations, creating photo opportunities for her as Kensington. Her image would be used on book covers, on his website, and in newspapers and magazines, anywhere Mac could arrange, all to promote the sale of the novels he had written, which he would retitle and launch under the name of this new storyteller. She would make herself available for radio and television shows as needed, and when it became important, she would go on a book tour and attend to all the other aspects of the press expected from a rising star. He would pay all the expenses, of course.

Elizabeth had some apprehension. It was a crazy idea. And what if the people she knew saw her in an advertisement or a news article, or in the event of success, on a book cover or a talk-show interview? And her boss? How would he react? But Mac was handy with answers and suggested she could simply tell her friends that she'd taken up writing and reinvented herself with a pseudonym. And still she might have told him no. She might not have done it, but there was something about the insistence of his wanting it to work out that swept her along. He was so full of enthusiasm about the possibilities, so full of hope about the success, that she found she couldn't refuse him. He also talked incessantly, badgering her with charm and invented rationale, until she acquiesced. The only snag was about a cut for her participation. Mac offered ten percent of the royalty, which she thought was slight. She countered with a third, but Mac was outraged. He wrote the novels, he was doing the outreach, the media relations, all the communications and marketing, and he would be negotiating the sales. He thought his offer was generous.

She didn't need the money. Her job paid a decent salary, and she wasn't sure the scheme would actually result in anything. In that case, she would have little invested, but if the plan did work, she'd have quite a lot to do and wasn't sure what impact it might have on her current livelihood. She was a mid-level administrator for a well-known insurance company in London that prized discretion as much as its rich clientele.

Things got a bit sharp when she insisted on a larger cut, and he likened her to a sex-worker at the brothel with whom he negotiated the week before. He wanted that girl to pretend to love him, and she demanded a premium. There was quite a row until the manager intervened and they agreed to a small increase in the fee. "And right she was," said Elizabeth, "proper pay for proper work."

"A man always pays for his relationships with women," Mac asserted, "and always more than is due." Elizabeth stared at him slightly offended and asked him why he felt as he did. Mac quipped back "Wife, mother, girlfriend, or whore, a man always pays and always pays more than he gets, because a man is stupid and believes his investment will pay off."

"You see relationships as an investment?" she asked.

"They are, aren't they?" he asked in return. "Money or not, you put in your time, yourself, and your heart, and you hope that what you put in pays off. You hope for love and loyalty, don't you? You have to believe that, or you would just stay home and never live." She blinked twice, saw his point, and they agreed on fifteen percent.

As they made their way to the café, in the magical light of the summer night, and with the glow from the local clubs crawling into the darkness of the walk, they did not see the man, staying in shadows, always a bit out of range, watching, his camera at the ready. Romance does that to people, the camera man thought, it makes them myopic. Only dealers in contraband and people with a finely-honed phobia of being found out keep a vigilant watch. The sleuth was glad that this was true. It made most people easier to catch.

———

————

CHAPTER 16
A Night of Wine and Music

When they arrived at the café, Ernesto welcomed them with open arms. Some of their local friends were on hand, and Ernesto's wife, Delores, made a special point to be there. Mac could see that Ernesto approved immediately. "She has the right blend of breeding and mistake," Ernesto said. "She will be your perfect author." And with that declaration, he opened one of his best bottles of wine, and everyone raised a toast to Elizabeth Kensington.

Elizabeth's actual surname was Schoenhauer. But Mac decided, long before, that his writer should not have an actual name. Besides, who would buy a paperback book written by a person named Schoenhauer? A dissertation on philosophy, or even a treatise of world economics maybe, but a detective novel, even one for fun? There wasn't a lot of fun in the name Schoenhauer and certainly no intrigue, except perhaps to wonder why someone did not change it.

But Mac considered thoughts other than the grace of the name. What complications could occur if the books were popular, and they bore the name of a real person? That might invite trouble. Since he intended fully for the plan to be successful, it was wiser to nip the bud of that possibility before it bloomed. A made-up name for a made-up author was the best choice. It left a lot of room for ambiguity if it became a litigious legal matter. Determining who was, or who is, is more difficult when no one is anyone.

Majorca Mac

The group at Ernesto's drank and drank and drank. The wine poured, and the music started. A three-person combo eked out sultry rhythms to underscore the fun and friendly conversation. There is something delicious about embarking on a lark with a touch of disingenuous larceny. It is sort of like lying about your past at a dinner party. There is a thrill that adds a layer to every moment, as if in the next second, the truth may be discovered, and the pretense will shatter into pedestrian reality.

Mac could take most things. Indeed, he survived most, but a pedestrian life was not something he was willing to have. Not ever again. He was no ordinary human being. He was filled with an unfulfilled and extraordinary destiny, and he would not let any truth keep him from it.

Elizabeth, perhaps not in the same definitive way, felt as he. It was a bit of a fairy story, a simple office girl coming for a holiday on the island of Majorca and finding her life transformed in a day. Not only was she a conspirator in a hilarious hoax, she was at the center of the light. Everyone wanted to know her. Everyone wanted to ask about her. Everyone wanted to dance with her. Never a beauty, attention did not come easily to Elizabeth's life. She was smart and handled herself well, but in life, attention is lavished on the ones who do not need it. It is almost never given to those who do. Not unless they made it happen. Not unless they held something to barter with or could trick everyone into feeling it was their due. Elizabeth had never been able to do that. She always refused to give up an ounce of her soul in exchange for insincere flattery. Nor did attention come her way naturally. Not before today. Not before this odd, older man walked over to the bench where she was sitting.

As the company shouted for dancers, couples took to the floor for a spin. The chant rose, "Elizabeth, Mac, Elizabeth, Mac!" Mac needed little persuasion; he enjoyed letting out his inner bacchanal. Extending an arm with a paso doblé flamenco stamp, he beckoned Elizabeth, and they danced to the approval of the crowd.

The flamenco music turned to salsa, then to samba, and finally to a slow seductive air, and Mac and Elizabeth danced, couples in the company joining them on the floor for their own intimate moments. Dance is more than movement to music. It is an arousal of spirit. Sometimes joyous, sometimes frantic, sometimes a simmer of what is kept hushed in your soul. It was surely the wine, the beautiful night, the spotlight, the warmth of companionship, and the acceptance felt from the group at the café, but Elizabeth and Mac moved as if there was love between them. More than the cling of an adolescent first dance, more than the press of hips in feverish hope, more than friends enjoying a night, there was an intimacy of two persons who understood each other and were conspiring together.

———————

CHAPTER 17
The Day After

The next morning, Mac woke in a rush of euphoria. Last night was a fantastic time. Everyone loved Elizabeth. She was a success. He loved the sound of that word. Success. All those "esses" together made it sensual and satisfying. She was a success; it was a success; he was a success.

He climbed out of the berth and made his way into the galley to start the morning coffee. The burner would not light. At first, he feared he may be out of propane but then remembered he'd been having trouble with the gas connector for several weeks. He would have to fix that. For this morning, he took a handy wrench from one of the galley cabinets, opened the door to the gas, and gave the tank a whack. He heard the gas flowing and started the coffee.

He used the head, taking time to brush his teeth and scrub his face. A shower would come after the caffeine. He heard the coffee percolating on the stove and went back to the galley. Then he spotted his newly purchased digital camera on the galley table and remembered all of the photos taken last evening. Now he wanted to see what moments he'd captured of the celebration.

The camera was sitting on top of the stack of rejection letters he had been collecting these past months. There would be no more of those. Not now, not with her. He thought to burn the letters, to scatter the ashes onto the sea, and let rejection drift away, but he stopped himself, thinking that having a reminder of the difficulty of the journey would add "esses" to the sweet soft success on its way.

He pushed buttons on the camera for several minutes, turning off the stove and pouring coffee as he worked. Why was a digital camera so difficult? They ought to make this easier, thought Mac, one simple magic button. Wouldn't that be better? One simple button, easy to find and easy to use. How hard could it be to create a camera with one single button? Finally, he stumbled onto the right combination to make the images appear on the camera screen, giving him a sense of accidental accomplishment, even if he wasn't certain he could recreate the sequence.

The first picture was of Elizabeth beaming with joy. The brim of her hat flopped along the side her face, and she was at once engaging and quirky. It was one of her greatest assets, Mac thought. She is beautiful from within, and a glimpse of her true quality was better than the most seductive model.

Next, was an image of her being toasted by the revelers. Everyone was smiling and looked so enthused. It was a great photo. Then came one of Elizabeth and Mac together at the bar drinking wine. Ernesto grabbed the camera, he guessed. He liked the photo. The writer and the literary agent hard at work. He could use that for the press as well.

The next was a photo of Mac and Elizabeth dancing the samba. They looked as if they were great friends. Maybe more. Mac liked the way he looked. He loved the way he danced the samba. Seeing the moment captured, the sheer joy of the experience came back to him, and he started dancing. He picked up the coffee, the camera, and his notebook and sambaed his way topside.

Once on deck, he inhaled sharply, tasting the uncorrupted air of the crisp morning and looked out at the coastline. Such beauty. He never tired of the view, but on this particular morning he responded to it more acutely than he did in a long while. What was different, he thought? Is the sky more blue? Is the water more aqua? Have the buildings along the coastline been repainted while he slept? No, he thought, it is hope that makes the colors richer. Hope adds hue. The color is in the observer's eye. And today his eye was on the color of opportunity.

Opportunity does not always present itself, that is important to remember. And when it does appear, it is only the fool who does not seize it. Here, with Elizabeth, was opportunity fallen within his reach, and he would seize it. He would act. He knew action was the mystical ingredient to change opportunity to success. He was almost as good at taking action as he was at talking.

And there was so much to do. Finding a perch and a place for his cup, he took his notebook and began to make a list. Two lists. One was a list of things he wanted to do to launch his new novelist, the other of repairs he would make on the boat. He jotted down the propane tank connector at the top of the list. The mast-rigging repair came next, and before ten minutes passed, there was a list of more than twenty on-board projects. When did the boat become so old, he wondered? He remembered he was harbored in Majorca for seven years. That is a long time for a boat to be moored. In that time a person may enjoy an easy and relaxed life of pleasurable pursuits, but a boat is like a young woman and does not like to sit without attention. It requires constant care and gentle caresses. When it has an ample amount of each, it sings when it sails. When it does not, it caterwauls.

The night before, after saying goodbyes to the friends at Ernesto's, he walked, well, staggered, but still escorted, Elizabeth back to the hotel in which she was staying. It was a modest place on the edge of the center of the tourist trade, nice enough, he was sure, but not a place a person of experience would book. An experienced traveler would have made a heartier choice. They said good night, sharing a handshake and an embrace, which is customary in the Mediterranean, and he headed back to the dock after agreeing to meet with her the next morning at ten-thirty to outline strategy. She was going to be on the island for only a week longer, and he wanted to make the most of the time as possible. Maybe, if the day was productive, he would look for a better accommodation for her. After all, she was no longer Elizabeth Schoenhauer; she was the prize-winning author Elizabeth Kensington. It was a business expense, he decided; a nice hotel would be a good background for holiday photos.

As full of ideas as his list was full of things to do, he went below to shower and dress and prepare for his action-packed day.

———

CHAPTER 18
And the Others

Elizabeth woke with a similar bewildering joy. Memories of the past night were surreal. For her, it was an out-of-character, if not an out-of-body, experience, and she felt akimbo as the reality of her modest hotel room and her thrifty holiday-clothes jarred with the fiery stardom of last evening.

There is a strange tension between the disparity of a wonderful dream and the realization of fact. Reality is a wonderful tragedy because it rarely lives up to expectations. And even on the unusual occasion that it does, isn't it a part of mankind's nature to always want more? Today was good, tomorrow will be better, and the next day will be staggeringly perfect. And then what? If a shopkeeper sells three items today, will they sell five tomorrow? And then seven the day after? Acceptance of the ordinary is an argument for mediocrity, isn't it?

Perpetual hope is guaranteed disappointment, but screw it, she thought. Today may, in fact, surpass all that have come before. History showed her that was likely untrue, but there is no payoff in constantly anticipating a downturn. That point of view is as insane as the other.

Besides, last night's adventure was a wonder. Today's may be equally so.

When she went to the restaurant in the lobby to order coffee and toast, she took the floppy hat that she wore last evening with her. She may not be an eccentric writer of best-sellers, but she could look it, especially in this place where she was unknown. Holidays are a bit of a dress-up, she thought. You can pretend to be whoever you want. Put on a hat, and you are famous. Perhaps it was the reflected glow from last night, or it may have been the hat, but she was certain that people in the restaurant were staring as if trying to place her as some celebrity they were sure they recognized.

* * * * * * * * *

Ernesto arrived at work early so he could clean up from last night's festivities. He liked Mac's discovery. Everyone did. If she went over as well with the book-buying public, the books, even if crap as Mac suggested, would be a big success. A big crap success.

What a world, Ernesto thought. Crap could be a money maker, and people were free to be whoever they wanted to be regardless of who they really were. Even Mac, he remembered. The lady tourist was a famous authoress, Mac was not himself, and the man with the camera was likely an international agent. He wondered why he was the only one who was still himself and taking out the empty bottles?

Maybe I'll be someone else as well, he thought. I could be a tarantella dancer. I have strong ankles, even if my stomach is a bit soft. Or I could play guitar in front of an open case on a popular corner of the promenade. Of course, he didn't play the guitar well, and gratuities would likely be limited to the short tourist season, which could make eating difficult. Or I could be a bar owner with a lovely wife, even if she was sometimes cross, and with beautiful children who loved him, even if he had to clean up the bar on the morning after parties. Maybe being me is just fine, he thought, and hoisted the trash to the bin.

* * * * * * * * *

The investigator, who was unofficial, stood on the promenade under the shade of a stout palm tree gazing toward Mac's boat. He took several photos of Mac standing on the boat's deck, taking in the view. He snapped as Mac climbed down the ship ladder, boarded his dinghy and headed toward the dock. He was capturing a photo with Mac at the helm, when the alert sounded on his phone, telling him that he received a text message. Shouldering his camera, he swiped the device and read: "Flight confirmed. Arriving Palma tomorrow eight a.m. Meet at hotel. Watch. M.M."

Tomorrow will be the day, he thought. Tomorrow it will be out of his hands. Tomorrow he'd be off to a new assignment, likely not as interesting. Back to the usual: Hunting cheating partners, getting evidence for unhappy people, and checking backgrounds for widows unsure of new romantic pursuers. No more disappeared bon vivants.

He spent several hours last night walking past the open door of the café and surreptitiously peeking in to sneak a look. It was a celebration. That he could tell. And it was something to do with the woman who came to the party with the sought-after father. Still he was uncertain what the cause of the merriment was. He started to ask one of the couples leaving but suddenly worried that intimate friends would be suspicious of questions, so he only asked the time.

Then the agent waited till the couple disappeared down the street, before he looked into the club again.

It looked like so much fun in there. All the dancing, all the joy, all the companionship. Much better than being in the shadows outside. He was always outside. He was always looking in, watching. He often wondered what it would be like to be on the inside, enjoying the fun and being a part of the action, instead of standing out of the light, watching through his camera and recording what others were living. He was so preoccupied with his thoughts that he didn't hear Mac approaching.

––––––––––

_____

CHAPTER 19
Mac Attack

Earlier when boarding the skiff, Mac noticed the light reflected from the lens of the camera on the shore. There was someone on the promenade taking photos. The camera seemed to be pointed in his direction, but the views of the bay were frequently the subject of shutterbugs, so he didn't give it much thought. Instead he motored to the dock to begin his errands.

When he tied up the dinghy and made his way to the promenade, Mac saw a man standing pensively with a cell phone in hand and an elaborate camera hung over his shoulder. Perfect, thought Mac, a real photographer. The photos taken with his newly purchased small camera were fine, but they were not of professional quality. They'd be useable for a blog post or an obscure site of celebrity spotting, but he would need professional shots of Elizabeth if he wanted people to pay attention. And here was life, presenting him with a perfect opportunity, a photographer with an extraordinary camera, right before him. He strolled down the promenade and made a beeline for the man.

"That is quite a camera you have," Mac said as he approached. The man was startled. He looked up with an odd expression of disbelief, as if he'd been discovered doing something he should not be doing.

"Yes. Yes. It's . . . it's a pretty good one," the man stuttered.

Mac wasn't sure why the man was so nervous. Perhaps he was taking closeups of some of the bikini clad sun-worshippers that gathered at the beach. "Are you a professional photographer?" Mac asked.

"Not really," the man stammered. "It's just a hobby."

"I bet that rig was expensive."

"It cost a bit." The man looked as if he were going to turn and go, but Mac was determined.

"What sort of lens is that?" Mac said. "I got this camera yesterday," he said showing his small digital camera, "and it is all right but nothing like that. I'll bet you can get some fantastic photos with that one."

"Well, it depends," the man said hesitating, "on what sort of photos you want."

"Are you here on holiday?"

"Yes, for a few days," the man replied.

"This will sound a bit forward, but I am wondering if you'd like to make a little money?"

The photographer was confused. What was this man up to? "Doing what?" he asked.

"Taking some photos," Mac said. "I am looking for a photographer to take a few photos. I came in from the water. I saw you, and I thought 'Why not ask?' My name is Mac. Mac McMartin." Mac put out his hand.

Of course, the investigator knew this was not true. He knew this man was Kevin MacNeal, who called himself Mac, but he couldn't tell him he knew. And it would be suspicious if he wasn't civil, so he took the extended hand and shook it. "I'm Dennis," he said.

"You're an American," Mac affirmed.

"Guilty," Dennis said.

"I am too. At least I was. I am from there. But I live here now. I have a boat out there." He pointed toward the bay. "A small boat."

Dennis knew the boat. He followed the café owner the day before and discovered the vessel in the harbor. The agent wasn't sure what Mac knew, so he was noncommittal. "That must be nice," Dennis said.

"Lots of work but cheaper than a hotel," Mac said. "Plus, you don't have to pack when you want to go somewhere else."

Easier to disappear into the ether as well, thought Dennis. "What sort of photos are you wanting?" Dennis asked.

"I know the most wonderful girl," Mac said intimately.

"I don't take those sorts of pictures," Dennis said.

"No, no, no — not that. I wouldn't mind having a few," Mac said, "but that's not what I have in mind. You see, I'm a literary agent," Mac spoke with conviction. "I represent writers — books, novels, film scripts — that sort of thing. And I'm about to launch an amazing new writer, Elizabeth Kensington. Have you heard of her?"

"No, I don't think so." Was that the woman at the center of the celebration last night, Dennis wondered? It was the same blonde he saw this man flirt with at this beach only yesterday. Hmm, a new writer.

"Well, you will," Mac said. "She's written this amazing new series about a detective involved in murder and marriage."

They often go together, Dennis thought.

"They are funny and really good – not just good, they are great. Anyway, I'll be representing her and her work, and she happens to be here in Majorca. Would you be available to take some photographs of her?"

Other than the ones I have, Dennis asked himself?

"I'd pay you of course. Not a huge amount, but something to add to your holiday funds. How much do you think you would charge?"

Dennis hesitated. He was mystified. The man he was hired to find and watch, to report on and take photos of, now wanted him to take photos for him. And this girl, the one the disappeared father met on the promenade, she's an emerging novelist — one who is about to be famous? And this man, the target of his search whose real name is Kevin MacNeal, is actually a literary agent who sails around the globe finding and recruiting star writers? And he is operating from a floating office aboard a beat-up boat moored off the coast of Majorca? The investigator could not wait to get to his hotel and check out this story on the internet. Imagine if he found link after link that verified the tale being told. Could it be the son, who hired him, didn't know of his father's new career? More likely, he thought, this was some scheme — to get the girl interested.

"Let me see if I understand. You want me to take photographs of your client, a lady who writes detective novels, and whose career you are promoting?" Dennis asked to be sure he was following.

"That's it," Mac said.

"And you'll pay me for my services?"

"Well, of course, subject to the results," Mac hedged, "and if we can actually use the photographs. A contingency agreement, will that work for you?"

Dennis knew he should say, "No." He already had a job, a job to keep track of this man till this man's son arrived. But there was nothing in his understanding with his client that said he couldn't keep track of the father by working for him, was there? The client indicated that the investigator should not approach the subject, but Dennis didn't. The subject approached him. And now that he'd been noticed, it would certainly be easier to keep track of him up close and personal rather than try to hide among the milling tourists. And undercover work is some of the most exciting you can do, he thought. And he'd take photographs and earn a little cash. It was all true. And it all sounded good and reasonable, but there was another thing that tugged at him with more strength than he could have expected: For once he'd be inside. He wouldn't be peeping into a window or through the lens of his camera. He'd be a part of it. He'd be a part of the action. And if the lady tourist could be a best-selling author, and the evaporated father could be a hustling literary agent, then why couldn't he be a photographer to the stars?

"Okay," he said, "I'll do it."

———

———————

CHAPTER 20
Photoshoot Plans

They spent another twenty minutes working on the details. Mac would pay thirty-five euros for each hour to be advanced against twenty-five euros for the rights to each photograph that Mac accepted. The negotiations were pretty simple. Mac was pleased that he got the photographer to work at such an affordable rate. That was another sign of the synchronicity of the meeting, Mac thought. The universe was conspiring to make this perfect. He knew the work would be fantastic, and the book would sell millions of copies. Everything was heading in the right direction.

Mac and the photographer agreed to meet at the cathedral at one p.m. Mac would bring the girl. Dennis would find a camera store and purchase a memory card that he would give to Mac at the conclusion of the day, after Mac paid him, of course. It was all settled, and they shook hands to seal the arrangement.

Dennis was oddly excited when he left to find a camera shop. It would only last a day, he thought. When the son arrives, the game is up. Either he would be outed, or he'd disappear into the smoke of the family fire. And although it might be on the borderline of professional ethics, he was looking forward to the afternoon. Maybe his life was due for a change. Maybe he'd been touched by the magic of Majorca.

Mac headed across town to Elizabeth's hotel. He was scheduled to meet her at ten-thirty a.m. for a strategy meeting, and he couldn't wait to tell her of this windfall. How easily that fell into place, he thought. Maybe this is what he was meant to do all along — be a literary agent. Conveniently, he forgot that Elizabeth Kensington was an administrator for a solicitor in London, and that she had not written a single word that wasn't on a legal memo.

———

―――――

CHAPTER 21
Across the Wire

"I'm flying to Majorca," Michael said after a minimal prerequisite hello.

"You are doing what?" the female voice asked on the phone.

"Majorca. Palma to be exact. It's on Majorca. That's a Spanish Island," Michael explained.

"I know what Majorca is," the woman said. "What I don't understand is why you are going?"

Michael took a split second to decide. Then he told her, "I am going to see our father. I am at the airport now, waiting for my flight to board."

"You are what?"

"I am going to see our father," Michael repeated.

"Are you crazy?" Beth shouted.

"Yes, I think I am," Michael replied.

"Why? Why would you want to see him?" Beth asked. "After all this time, after what he did, the way he treated Mom, and us, and then disappearing without so much as a Christmas card. What is wrong with you?"

"Unfinished business."

"Are you planning to shoot him?" Beth asked drolly.

"Ha, ha, ha. I'd laugh myself to the floor, but it might create a scene on the concourse," Michael retorted.

"Why would you want to drag it all up again?" Beth nagged. "All that dirt. I have spent years in therapy trying to forgive. Leave the scab alone. Let the scar heal."

"I just want to hear him say it," Michael said.

"Well, don't hold your breath," Beth said. "It has been years, and there hasn't been a peep."

"I'm going. I'll be there tomorrow morning," Michael told her.

"How did you find him?" Beth queried.

"A misintended letter and a private investigator."

"An investigator? You hired a private investigator to find him?" Beth was astonished.

"Yes."

"That's a pretty big investment," Michael's sister pointed out.

"I couldn't locate him without help."

"Mind boggling," Beth sneered. "This is all beyond my ability to understand. You haven't mentioned this to our brother, have you?"

"No."

"Well, don't," Beth said curtly. "I've learned to live with the shame, but if Jonathan knew what you were up to, you'd send him running one more time. And Mother, thank God she's dead. This would push her over."

"You have a great way of pointing out silver linings," Michael responded.

"Look, Father didn't even attend the funeral service. Do you remember?" Beth asked pointedly.

"I am not standing up for him," Michael insisted. "I just want some — I don't know — satisfaction."

"You are over fifty years old; satisfaction is a rare commodity."

"While bitchiness is in abundance," Michael said sardonically.

"An animal learns to bite with experience," Beth hissed. Michael sighed. He knew Beth would be a stone. "I just don't see the point," she went on. "He stole our time, our childhood, our family, our mother, and most of the money. Do you expect to reason with him?"

"I don't know. A part of me wants to kick him in the teeth," Michael conceded.

"Aim a little lower for me, Brother."

"Don't you ever wonder?" Michael asked.

"'No," Beth replied sharply. "I don't even know who he is, some wannabe globe-trotter chasing a sunset and a woman, I am sure. People don't change, you know. No one does. They just become more of themselves."

"The good gets better, and the bad gets worse?" he summarized.

"No one gets better, Michael. We all decay," Beth declared.

There's the cheery Beth he tried so hard to ignore. As long as he could remember, she was hard as flint. Dad attributed it to their mother's German heritage. He often said his wife was cold and heartless. Michael never saw those qualities in the woman who bore him, but he could certainly see them in his sister. He tried to make allowances; she went through a difficult time, but he never thought that her being nasty helped. "Listen, they are calling my flight. I have to go to the boarding ramp," Michael announced.

"Yeah, yeah, you don't want to miss the flight. Listen, when you see the fuck, don't mention me, all right? He won't ask about me, I'm sure. And if he does, tell him I died." She hung up.

Families are the ties that bind, Michael thought. In some cases, you are hog-tied and gagged. Maybe that was why he wanted to go, he thought, to be set free.

—————

————

CHAPTER 22
Angry Woman

When Beth finished talking to her brother, she hung up with more irritation than she could have imagined. What was he up to, she wondered? Her brother was always a steadfast person, choosing order and rational behavior over whim. Michael was the substitute patriarch of the family. He steered them through the choppy sea after their parents' exodus and kept the candle burning when their mother extinguished from cancer. It was completely out of character for him to go off like this. She decided to forget that he called, much less for such an inane subject as an around-the-world treasure hunt for a dissipated progenitor. She wouldn't give it another thought. That was about the amount of thought she felt her father gave her.

She tried to go about her day, which was always filled to the minute with completely pointless projects. But today, despite the direction she moved, she was overwhelmed with anxiety. Why? What was the point? What was her brother up to? She would need some therapy to think this one through. Therapy for Beth, at this point in time, was opening a bottle of wine and pouring herself a large glass. From the corner of her eye, she caught sight of the living room wall clock. It was already eleven a.m. She applauded her restraint. Usually she started drinking by ten. She didn't drink a lot, she told herself, only a little. Three or four glasses during the day wasn't bad. There was a time when the number was greater. But she cut way back.

For a while she didn't drink at all. She took up binge eating instead. She went through cake faster than an overweight groomsman at a wedding reception. And pies. She could eat an entire ten-inch pie in an hour. Of course, her weight ballooned up and up and up until her husband, David, finally asked what was going on. He said that he was worried for her, but she didn't believe him. She knew the truth: He didn't like fat women. She started purging after that.

Besides, drinking wine as therapy wasn't as bad as some remedies she'd tried. The scotch left her motionless. It was hot and sharp when it slid down her throat, giving her a glow and inspiring her to dance to a blaring stereo. She'd move and groove and bump and shake until she'd run out of steam, and then she'd collapse on the sofa and sleep.

The chocolate brought her to the edge of diabetes, but it was easier to hide. Sometimes, she'd sneak outside on the precept of taking a walk and eat candy bars she kept stashed in her car. Sometimes, she'd get shakes from the sugar, but shakes are easier to hide than weight. And as long as she didn't eat much at meals, it wasn't noticeable.

Now, she sat in her favorite chair, with her legs curled up and the stemmed wineglass in her hand. She sipped, waiting for the wine to soothe the jagged edges she felt in her stomach, and she thought. They were not gentle simple thoughts, but ones with razor-sharp edges.

———

————

CHAPTER 23
Wardrobe and All

When Mac arrived at Elizabeth's hotel, she was waiting in the lobby. She sat on one of the matching sofas, thumbing through a glossy magazine. She sat squarely, with her legs crossed, and Mac was once again taken by the ease and composure with which she held herself. He knew better than to accept what he saw at face value, but if he was betting, he would have given two-to-one that she never lost her cool. Elizabeth Kensington would have just that same poise. She would be calm in battle, gracious under fire, and have a quiet amusement that comes from knowing she will be victorious. Elizabeth looked up and smiled. They planned breakfast at the hotel restaurant, but when he told her about the latest development, she stopped.

"A photoshoot? Today? But my hair, my make-up, my clothes," she protested.

"It will be impromptu," Mac said.

"Improvisation leaves a lot to chance," Elizabeth said. "Chance is as often a friend to failure as it is to success. Let's alter the odds in our favor. What time are we meeting?"

"One o'clock," Mac stated.

"And it's nearly eleven now. Let's get to work." And off she whisked him in the direction of the elevator. "Of course, you do understand that taking you upstairs in the middle of the morning will compromise my reputation at this hotel, don't you?" she teased.

"Scandal is good for your character," Mac pronounced. "It adds a layer of mystery."

"In that case, put your arm around my shoulder." Mac was happy to oblige, and as suspected, the desk clerk lowered his eyes as they passed.

Upstairs in her room she worked like the wind. She collected her make-up from the bathroom counter and stored it in a case. She snatched up a hairbrush and a tube of something guaranteed to sooth the unruliest of manes, and then opened the door of the closet and began pulling out possible outfits.

"What do you think of this?" she'd ask Mac, and before he could even answer, which ultimately would have been no use at all for he did not have a taste for fashion, she'd pitch it aside with comments of it being "too conservative," or "too flashy," or "a bad color."

"What about the little summer dress you wore last night?" Mac suggested.

"It may be less than fresh," Elizabeth said.

"Doesn't the hotel have a quick service?" he asked.

"We'll ask. If not, we'll spray it with cologne and hope no one notices."

There were several lovely scarfs in her holiday luggage, but a nice professional blazer was missing from her wardrobe. She'd left anything even remotely resembling business at home. The solution to the problem seemed obvious to both; they would need to shop. Snatching up her newly found signature hat and her handbag, she and Mac headed out of the hotel and to the nearby shop-lined Paseo del Borne.

Paseo del Borne is the center of upscale retailers in Palma. The quiet street with a canopy of trees and cafés opening onto the pavement is home to some of the world's most famous names in fashion. In earlier years the area was a down-trodden roadway of unrecognized stores and casual drinking establishments, but as Palma embraced international stores, and tourists with stashes of cash flocked to the city, the area transformed into the current pricey thoroughfare. Now, Louis Vuitton, Hugo Boss, Massimo Dutti, and H & M are just a few of the brands that adorn the street where Mac and Elizabeth found themselves. It took only two stores for them to find the perfect jacket. It was navy blue, made of light wool, and fit perfectly. Mac, who prided himself on creating the perception that he lived without financial limitations, balked at the price, but Elizabeth said not to worry. They would leave the tags on the blazer and return it after the shoot. Unless she fell in love with it, in which case she'd take it with her. The blazer could be a functional memento. There is nothing wrong with sentimentality, she thought, as long as it is practical. After leaving the shop, with the new jacket in hand, they swept by the hotel, picked up her garment bag and makeup case, and then headed toward the cathedral.

————

CHAPTER 24
The Fun Begins

Dennis was waiting at the cathedral when the duo arrived. He obtained a memory card from a camera store near his hotel and purchased a collapsible circle-reflector for bouncing light, which he read was essential for taking good portraits. It was a whimsical purchase, but he always wanted one, and this seemed like a perfect opportunity.

Even with the shopping, there was enough time for him to check the internet. There wasn't much to find. As he suspected, there was no listing for either Mac MacNeal, literary agent, or Elizabeth Kensington, rising novelist. He wondered what they were up to. It seemed clear to him that whatever folly was afoot, Mac was the mastermind. Never having been an instigator of plans, Dennis held a certain appreciation for this man's eccentric insistence.

Thinking that some wardrobe changing might be needed, Dennis arranged to use a small room by the side door of the cathedral for dressing. When the woman arrived with bags in hand, he was glad for the intuition. Elizabeth thanked him for his kindness, and Mac, thrilled with Dennis' ingenuity, kept congratulating himself on how clever he was to spot the asset. After introductions, they trudged, bags in hand, up the stairs to the place of worship and the makeshift changing room, with Mac promising to light a candle in Dennis' honor.

For the next hour Dennis fussed over Elizabeth as if he had been shooting celebrity photographs for a lifetime. "Tilt this way," he said, or "Lift your chin." "Look into the camera." "Smile as if you have a sexy secret."

Mac was beaming. "How long have you been doing this?" he asked Dennis.

"It feels as if I've just started," Dennis replied.

"She has that effect on me too," Mac concurred and then started adding his two cents to the photo direction. "Coquette." "Grin." "Move to the left." The double-sided direction didn't divert Elizabeth, she went one way and then the other, accommodating all instruction with ease and wonderful poise. Neither did Dennis acknowledge any sense of over-stepped boundaries. On the contrary, he seemed to enjoy the collaboration saying, "Oh, yes," or "Perfect," to the comments tossed in. Often, they'd laugh at a moment they found funny. Like when Elizabeth was caught unawares with her mouth open in protest, or when an unsuspecting tourist stepped into the frame. At one point, Elizabeth said she felt like a show pony being put through its paces. Dennis responded by saying that, to the camera, she didn't look horsey at all.

They took photos of Elizabeth sitting on the cathedral stairs, standing at the cathedral door, facing the cathedral with her arms up, and looking out over the city below. There were closeups, scenic shots, shots from the waist up; photo after photo after photo, but none of the trio resented the effort. A person passing by would have seen three friends who were enjoying a camera-clicking lark rather than strangers whose paths just crossed.

After hundreds of photos, they retrieved their belongings from the cathedral changing room and started down the steps. As they approached the bay, Mac suggested photographs on the water's edge, but Dennis already prepared a list of locations and led them first to the Café La Lonja, where a table and wine were waiting.

After arranging the light to the best advantage, Dennis took some stills of the lady author sipping, sniffing, toasting, and peering over the glass of wine. In a moment of inspiration, Mac took a handful of euros from his pocket and corralled a group of nearby children, who surrounded Elizabeth for impromptu autographs and fan photos. After graciously tipping the café manager and offering a token of appreciation to the waiter who gave up his table for the event, the trio crossed to the fountain in the Plaza de la Reina and took photos of Elizabeth playing in the water. With only slight urging, she took off her shoes and stood in the water a la Anita Ekberg in "La Dolce Vita." Mac applauded the creativity, and Dennis clicked away, catching the moments of joy, until a local policeman wandered toward the scene. With apologies, and supported by Dennis' extended hand, Elizabeth stepped out of the waters of the fountain and back to earth.

"Who's hungry?" Mac asked and refusing to accept any decline, they sat as a group outdoors at a nearby eatery and ordered a mid-afternoon bite. Periodically throughout the meal Dennis asked Elizabeth questions.

"How did you meet?" "Have you been writing for a long time?" "How did you start?" At first, Elizabeth was vague, brushing off the inquires or deferring to Mac for information. Eventually, she got the drift of Mac's answers and started adding details or even correcting him of errors in their history.

Dennis knew the biographical information was being conjured, but he simply didn't care. He was having too much fun being a part of the charade. The most awkward moment came when Mac went off to pay the bill, and Dennis asked about the new book.

"Oh, it's one of those stories," Elizabeth replied. "Boy gets girl, boy loses girl, boy is accused of murder."

"Does it work out?" Dennis asked.

"You'll have to wait for the book," Elizabeth cooed.

After paying the lunch bill, Mac returned to the table with one of the busboys, who was holding the small camera Mac purchased "Come on, let's get together," Mac said moving a chair between Dennis and Elizabeth and drawing them close. He wanted a photo. Dennis thought for a brief second that maybe that was not a good idea.

"You don't want a photo of me," Dennis insisted. "I'm a nobody."

"A picture of us all together would be history," Mac said indicating the small camera he'd brought. "I've been taking photos all day, but none of the three of us. One day, you may be famous as the photographer of the best-selling author Elizabeth Kensington, and I want to prove I was there."

Considering there was no Elizabeth Kensington, Dennis could not imagine that dream would come true, but on the other hand, he couldn't think of any way to voice a concern without raising questions, so he smiled giddily as the busboy took the picture.

"One more photograph," Mac announced, "just one." He led them back to the promenade, to the bench where he and Elizabeth first met. That was also the first time Dennis saw them together. "Here," Mac said, indicating the bench, and then he sat next to Elizabeth, posing with a smile of pride, as Dennis retroactively immortalized the meeting.

"Well, that's it," Dennis said, "unless you can think of anything?" Agreeing there was plenty to work with, Dennis pulled the memory card from the camera and gave it to Mac.

"Thank goodness," Elizabeth said. "Now, I can go back to the hotel and soak in a hot tub all night."

"What about the dancing?" Mac beseeched.

"My feet are killing me," Elizabeth said. "There must be a rule about this in our contract."

"You are absolutely correct," Mac exclaimed. "Let's dispatch for a siesta and then meet again at eight p.m. How does that sound?"

"That sounds divine," Elizabeth capitulated.

"Dennis?" Mac turned to the photographer, who looked surprised and a bit confused. "You'll be joining us, won't you?"

"Aren't we finished?" Dennis proposed.

"With work, yes. But this is for fun. Why don't you come with us? After today, something would be missing if you don't."

Dennis experienced a sensation he didn't remember feeling before. He felt accepted. They wanted him to be a part of the celebration. He paused for a moment to phrase a response, but Mac jumped in.

"We're going to a little place I know in the Old City. It's nothing elaborate just a great time with great people. A friend of mine owns it. Ernesto's."

Dennis knew the place, of course. He asked there about Mac. He followed them to the place the night before. He stood outside the establishment, while Mac and Elizabeth danced, and he peered into the café for glances while walking by in his tourist persona. Now . . . now . . . he was wondering what the owner would say if he appeared there. Perhaps the man wouldn't even recognize him. Still, it might be better not to tempt fate.

"I'm sorry," Dennis said. "I have another engagement."

"Break it," Mac insisted.

"I can't," Dennis regretted. "I'll have to take a rain check."

"Oh, what a shame," Mac said, reaching out to give Dennis a hug. "It won't be the same, but we'll do our best to celebrate your absence, won't we Elizabeth?"

"We will have a drink in your honor to commiserate our loss," she said and hugged Dennis gratefully, kissing him on his cheek.

Fees paid, and handshakes concluded, Mac once again clapped the photographer on the back, and the three parted company. Mac and Elizabeth walked back to her hotel, Mac acting as porter. He would head back to the boat for a rinse and his favorite samba shirt before meeting with his new wordsmith for the nighttime celebration. Dennis watched as Mac and Elizabeth walked away. He was overwhelmed by a true sense of loss.

———

CHAPTER 25
Regrets and Ruminations

Thirty-five thousand miles above the North Atlantic, Michael sat in his business-class seat, wishing the atomic teleporter had already found its way from science fiction to household use. Even in his roomy seat and after three drinks, he still could not get settled. Echoes of his conversation with Beth reverberated in his mind.

Why? Why? Why? What did he want from his father? He didn't know. He sat with the noise of the jet engines and the occasional snore of one of the luckier passengers and tried to envision the reunion. How would his father look in real life? Would he sound like an old man? Would he be as irritating as Michael remembered?

Beth said no one changes. Michael wondered if that was true. Somewhere inside, he hoped she was wrong. He didn't expect an enthusiastic kill-the-fatted-calf welcome, but — what? Kindness? Gratitude? Warmth? Warmth from his father? He thought back through memories of his younger years. Did he ever know warmth from his father? Michael laughed ruefully, drawing the attention of his seatmate who glanced up from the movie on his laptop and removed the earbud to look inquiringly. Michael shook his head in apology and put his head on the pillow at the side of his seat.

What did he remember about his father? He remembered his father was always working. When his father wasn't at his business working, he was working on the house or the yard. On holidays, he'd sometimes bar-b-que, but even that was work. That was how his father viewed everything: Work. And his father preferred to be left alone when he was working. Even when the children were assigned chores, they were always sent off to work on their own. He couldn't remember them ever doing a group project with their father. Michael supposed there must have been hugs and fatherly advice, but he couldn't recall the moments. Even on the rare occasions when the family went en masse to a campsite or picnic area, Michael could remember little of his father that he'd classify as warmth.

His father was of a different generation. Michael understood that. Affection between a father and son wasn't considered good parenting. It was considered unmanly. It was as if kindness would weaken the child. A father's job was to provide food and shelter, not love. You went to mom for sympathy and love. And even on the infrequent moments when he went to his father for caring, his father seemed put upon and uncomfortable.

Michael remembered one day he wanted to talk to his father about a problem he was having with one of the fellow students at school. The kid, a year ahead of him, for no apparent reason, started picking on him, calling him stupid and pudgy. His father was in the middle of fixing a closet pole in one of the bedrooms. When Michael asked if he could talk to him, his father said, "Michael, can't you see I am in the middle of fixing this? Ask your mother" Michael could remember the sting of that moment even now. Right then, Michael decided he would not be like his father. He would not be dismissive. He would treat his children with love and not keep pushing them away. He would take time to be with his children, to let them know they were loved and cherished.

But now, sitting in the seat of the airplane, he recalled many times when he told his own children he was too busy for them. He could remember saying to his own son, "Can't your mother help?" He remembered telling his daughter that he did not have time for her. He promised he would not be like his father, but he was doing exactly what his father did. Life takes a lot to live and finding time to live with love is a challenge that requires dedication. His father was not dedicated to that challenge. Maybe Michael also lacked that dedication. Maybe it is not possible for any parent to rise to the level of dedication needed.

As an adult, Michael remembered walking down a street one day and seeing his father in the reflection of a store window. He was startled, but when he turned to look, he saw it wasn't his father. It was him. He never noticed how much he looked like his father. He remembered several occasions when he heard himself saying simple phrases that were trademarks of his own father. "It won't get done by itself." "Everything takes upkeep if you want it to last." It is an eerie and horrifying feeling for a son to realize he has become his father. Maybe that's why Michael wanted to find him. Maybe he wanted to see his future, or maybe he wanted to tell his father that he was responsible for making Michael what he was. Or . . . ? How long was this damn flight, he thought, and then he drifted into a semi-unconscious state.

———

―――――――

CHAPTER 26
Siesta

Mac went back to his boat and took a quick nap. When he raised himself, he powered up his computer and fed the memory card into the reader. They ought to have these memory cards for people, Mac thought. You could download whole pieces of your history, clear your brain, and then upload them by the year for a stroll down hard-drive memory lane. Wouldn't that be convenient, he thought? Take out the bad things and eliminate the possibility that unpleasant memories might surface at unpredictable moments. Gone were the disgruntled sighs, the accusatory stares, the overbearing wife, the angry children. What was left was — success — the computer blinked, the images of the day appeared on the screen, and there was Elizabeth. How happy she looked sitting on the cathedral steps with that silly hat flopping around the side of her face and making her look irresistible.

He advanced through the images, slowly at first, then with increasing speed, much like a child at a toy store, discovering impossible joy at every turn. These were good, he thought, exceptional. He was certain these photographs would capture the attention of editors and newspapers everywhere. Then he stopped. Staring at him from the screen was a candid photo. The camera was pointed toward Mac, striking some clownish fashion-model pose. In the background, he could see Elizabeth watching. But she wasn't watching, she was staring at Mac, and with a look of — what was it? Desire? Admiration? Assessment? Amusement? Intrigue? Delight? Affection? And suddenly Mac wondered — does she love me? Is that what he saw in her eyes? Is that what she was feeling in the photograph? It wasn't ambivalence; that he could tell. And then he looked more closely at the images and wondered: Do I have feelings for her?

* * * * * * * * *

Mac was not the only one looking at the luminescent images of the lady with the floppy hat. Dennis surreptitiously copied the photos onto his own memory card before handing the one in the camera to Mac. He felt a little sheepish about the duplicity, but he never said Mac could have the only copies. He rationalized that this was not really trickery, but a way he could study the photographs and learn how he might improve his photographic technique. As an investigator he did a lot of things with his camera that might be considered marginally ethical, but he always brushed it off as necessary, a part of the job. Even as he copied the card, he felt a pang of conscience, and that was before the invitation to the evening at Ernesto's. That invitation elevated his sense of smuttiness. He was caught between his deception and his desire. Oh well, he thought, don't think too much of it. Tomorrow morning the mask will slide off anyway.

His attention returned to the photographs. They were good: The lighting, the temperatures, the composition — effective — and they captured Elizabeth in her multi-faceted sparkle. He often wondered how the camera could contain the energy of a moment. He understood it was mechanical, and that the photographer only contrives to capture an image that makes the viewer feel the specialness of the moment. Yet somehow, the camera captured more than a moment. It captured the spirit. He never understood it.

Even in the unobserved candid photos, which were the majority of his side-long view of the seamier side of relationships, there was some incomprehensible essence. He took squalid pictures of husbands emerging from mistresses' apartments, businessmen meeting to sell secrets, and fathers stalking stolen children. But still, there was some fundamental quality that existed in the documentary-styled photography. The photos taken today, without concern or wariness, without hiding to capture, or skulking for evidence, were managed at artistic levels rivaling the early days of his education. Maybe photography was his passion. Maybe he sold out his true dreams. Maybe this was what he was really meant to do.

One photograph of Elizabeth on the cathedral stairs, looking toward the lens of the observer, revealed more intimacy than any of those he ever took from the shadows. In that photograph, you could see her soul. You could see into her heart. What a surprising and incredible day. Why did they have to ruin it by asking him to go with them to the bar?

* * * * * * * * *

Elizabeth was exhausted when she got back to her hotel room. It was a whirlwind day. Running here, running there, changing her clothes four times. What a lot of energy it took to be a celebrity, she thought. How do film stars keep it up? She dropped her things on any available spot and went directly to the bath to draw a tub. With

104

the water running, she went back to the bedroom, kicked off her shoes, and took off every stitch she was wearing. She looked up, saw herself in the full-length mirror at the side of the room, and gave herself an appraising eye. Not bad, she thought, mostly still firm, only a slight sag here and there. She turned sideways. A little too round in a few places and not quite round enough in others. Not bad, but not great. She snatched her robe and put it on, covering any perceived inadequacy before returning to the bathroom to check the tub. She went back to the bureau in the bedroom and poured a glass of wine, then once again she went into the bath, gave the water the toe-test, and happy with the results, hung the robe on the door and stepped into peaceful bliss.

Displaced fragments, images of the past two days, crowded her mind — posing, the camera, dancing at the café, the faces of the children at the table, the first meeting with Mac — all the shards were passing in random order at hyper-hypnotic speed. She sipped on the wine and tried to breathe calmly to slow down the rhythm of her thoughts and allow them to drift off into the water.

Eventually, she began to relax, and she could reconstruct the memories of the day more easily and more slowly. The interest in seeing Mac again. Waiting in the lobby to find out what the day would bring. Then Mac's arrival and suddenly being pressed into action by the announcement of the photos. It was fun, she thought, but why did Mac plan it at the last moment? Greater advance notice would have been useful. Having to pull herself together in a flash and trudge all over the town to make faces at a camera was quite a lot to expect. She missed the trip to the castle she organized. Yes, playing dress-up was vigorous fun, but if it was such a lark, why was she so exhausted?

And agreeing to another boisterous outing that night? Why did she agree? It is true, she adored dancing, but still . . . She would have to be sure to keep the evening's adventures in hand. Sometimes, lovely and calm is just as captivating as bombastic and bold, she thought. People who take a vacation for rest and relaxation often drive themselves to manic activity, only to discover when they return home, they are worn out. Tonight, she would try to inject restraint and sensibility — that would be hard with Mac, she thought. He is like one of those engines that goes faster and faster with each moment, cannibalizing everything it encounters and propelling it to jet speed. He is a turbine, without a regulator.

It is a charming quality in a man. And yes, she thought it many times; he is charming. But wouldn't it be wonderful if he were charming and calm simultaneously? She slipped a little lower into the water, hoping the hypnotic effect of his personality would dissolve. Then suddenly, she opened her eyes and thought: That damned jacket. I have to remember to return that damned, over-priced, blue blazer first thing in the morning.

* * * * * * * * *

Ernesto worked through the afternoon, but not with his usual diligence. He did not hear from his friend, Mac, and was worried that something was not right. Of course, Mac was with the new senorita and was probably busy showing her the town, but still Ernesto wished his friend would stop by if for no other reason than to ease his concerns. It was extremely selfish of Mac not to consider the anxiety of his friend. He would remember to tell Mac that, when he finally visited. In the meantime, Ernesto unpacked the boxes that were delivered, restocked the bar, and mopped the floor of the café. But even with the distraction of the daily chores, he could not stop wondering.

Mac had been taking care of himself for a long time. Ernesto watched him go through many changes: Ups and downs, rants and raves, dreams dashed and hopes reborn. He saw Mac with many different women, all of them of the professional variety. But last evening, watching Mac with the blonde, Ernesto thought he saw something more. That worried him. As strong as he knew Mac to be, he wasn't sure how his friend would survive heartbreak.

———————

CHAPTER 27
Locked and Loaded

Beth spent most of the day drinking and thinking. What started as a distraction, after the call from her brother, turned into a preoccupation. What was her brother up to? Was this some part of a twelve-step program her brother started without saying anything? Accuse the father and earn ten points toward eternal redemption? Or was it a plan for revenge? Get even, get out. Or a patricide? Maybe he was planning an Oedipus thing without the marrying part?

Michael hired a private investigator to find their father. That showed a lot of commitment. Her brother must have something specific in mind. He was vague on the phone, saying he didn't know why he was going. That did not sound like Michael at all. Michael never made a move without a reason. Why didn't he tell her what it was when she'd asked? What game was he playing?

Several times, she tried to dismiss the conversation. She went to the sunroom with her pruning shears to trim the dying fronds from her favorite potted fern. Beth liked it when visitors commented on how beautiful the plant was, or asked if it was artificial, and then marveled at how well maintained it was. She started snipping fronds and began imagining she was removing her father's man-parts. In the past, the thought of paternal neutering gave her great satisfaction, but today, after a few snips, she abandoned the shears and focused on the mystifying news that Michael was flying to see Father.

She went into her dressing room to reorganize her underwear drawers. It was a task that gave her fulfillment. She liked to see things neatly organized and enjoyed making them that way. That was a gift from her mother. "Love is order," her mother would often say. "When things are tidy, they are easier to love." Beth did not know if that was true, but arranging her clothing always seemed to help. Not this morning. She folded and tucked her undies into their proper place, but her questions about Michael's motives kept nagging at her until she tossed everything into the chest haphazardly.

At about noon, and with three or more glasses of wine under her belt — in fact, she lost count — she realized she hadn't eaten, so she foraged for food. Typically, she avoided lunch, preferring to nibble just enough to keep her on task. She found some cheese in the refrigerator and a package of exquisite gourmet deli-crackers and made herself a small plate. She was sure that would keep her upright. And it did, for a while. Then she decided a short lay-down was in order. But there is no rest for a mind on a mission.

As she lay on her bed, she knew something was not right. Michael was not flying off for no reason. Maybe her father was terminally ill? It was a long time since she saw him, and he was older. Maybe he developed cancer or cirrhosis of the liver. That wouldn't surprise her, given what she remembered of his taste for drinking. Still, wouldn't it be easier to say, "Sorry you're dying and screw you?" But Michael was flight-bound, and Majorca is a long distance to go just to give the old man a kiss-off. There must be something more.

The property was all sold off when the parents sailed. There was a little money, but they divvied it when Mother passed. Unless there was more somewhere. Something Father did not disclose. There was that woman, Beth remembered. That secretary or whatever she was. Susan, Sandy. Some "S" name. That woman helped her father with lots of business things, bookkeeping and stuff. Thinking of it, Beth realized Father took a lot of effort to keep that woman's name out of family conversation. What was it? Sarah? Sophie? Maybe Michael knew her. Maybe that secretary still worked for Father on the sly. Maybe with her help, Dad stashed a bundle out of reach. That must be it. Michael talked to the woman and found out there was a trove. Ms. "S"-whatever must have said something, even without knowing she did, that tipped Michael off. Her brother discovered that Father tucked a chunk away, and now he was going to Majorca to stake his claim and squeeze out the other siblings. What a shit!

It was so like Michael to keep everything for himself. Even as a child, he would take the largest slice of cake or hide the cookies to make sure there was plenty for him. And now, here he was again, making sure he got the lion's share, if not all, of what he discovered was secretly put aside. Well, screw him if he thought he could get away with it. She'd take him to court. She'd raise a ruckus among the family. She'd make certain he didn't make her look like a moron.

When her husband returned from work at four-thirty p.m., the house was quiet. David called out Beth's name from the hallway, and when there was no reply, he went to the patio, a favorite place for a late afternoon nip. But the patio, like the house, held no Beth. Perplexed, if not yet alarmed, he made his way into the kitchen.

There on the tablet next to the phone was a hastily scrawled note: "Am flying to Spain."

———

———

CHAPTER 28
A Walk Across the Starry Night

Mac dressed with more care than usual. He spent extra time shaving and even clipped the miscellaneous hairs that grew in places where twenty-five years ago they never appeared. He put on a pair of ivory linen pants, a clean T-shirt, and his favorite samba shirt. The shirt was decades old and was faded to a soft patina of red with a tropical print. When he danced, the shirt flowed with his movement and made him feel sexy. Now all he needed was his secret weapon.

Living on board a ship, especially one as small as Mac's, leads to inventiveness. Things are stored anywhere they can be secured; under galley benches, above bunks, even under the floor of the hold. The trick is to remember where the things you want are consigned. You think it would be easier to locate miscellaneous extravagances because there are fewer places to look. But the opposite is true. Having everything stashed makes it more difficult to find the exact item you want, especially when you don't often hunt for a special treasure. Mac stood in the galley and surveyed the options. Where was it? He lifted one of the seat benches but did not find what he was looking for. He slid open the compartment under the bunk and found no success there. He finally remembered and looked into the back of the food cabinet. There, tucked behind the strapped canister of flour and next to the backup box of salt, he found the prize, a small bottle of men's cologne called "Midnight Magic." It was a gift from his first wife for their eighteenth anniversary. He hoped it was still useable. Nothing is worse than going to a rendezvous with a disagreeable smell. He opened the bottle to check, and the fragrance was still wonderful. The cologne was expensive, and he only used it on rare occasions. He dabbed a drop onto his palms and patted it into his cheeks. He loved exquisite things. This smell was reserved for the most anticipated moments. Properly scented and after checking his appearance in the mirror, he grabbed his wallet, watch, and the small camera and headed topside to make the trek across the evening water. On deck, he stopped to take in the clear evening air and was surprised to find he was shaking a little. He didn't know why, but he was nervous. Maybe that is a good sign, he thought.

Mac and Elizabeth met at the fountain that only a few hours ago served as a background for their frolics. After telling each other how nice they looked — Mac complimenting her evening floral dress, and Elizabeth admiring his samba shirt — Mac extended his arm, she took it, and they walked together across the Old City, heading toward Ernesto's.

The walk was pleasant, but they were quiet. They'd glance at one another from time to time as they strolled and say something about the moonlight, or the temperature, most of which they already said. The bantering conversation so present on previous occasions was replaced with an almost tentative atmosphere. The lights of the restaurants and cantinas they passed created an exciting backdrop of color against the darkened streets. But neither of them noticed the festive, if contrived, atmosphere.

All adventures have that arc, Mac thought. There is a point when carefree abandonment is infected by concern. It changes things. Lust is easiest when it is confined to body parts, and love is simplest when you don't give a damn about what happens. Once even the slightest hint of true feelings enters, it all changes.

Elizabeth must have felt something was on Mac's mind. When they arrived at the corner of the street that housed Ernesto's café, she stopped. "Are you all right?" she asked.

"A beautiful night, a beautiful woman, how could anything not be right?"

"What does it mean when a man answers your question with another question?" Elizabeth replied.

"That he is caring and curious," Mac said.

"And that he has something on his mind," Elizabeth stated. "Are you having second thoughts about the book?"

"No," Mac insisted. "It will be a huge sensation. I cannot wait."

"Perhaps you have thought of someone who would be more suited to represent your writer?"

"Absurd," Mac refuted. "You are Elizabeth Kensington."

"Then what is it?" Elizabeth persisted. "There is something. I can feel it. Tell me now, before we go any further, or I am going back to my hotel for a quiet night of pay-per-view."

Mac experienced tougher positions, but none made him feel as he did now. Typically, when he was confronted by the force of any feeling, or when he was overcome by a burning desire, especially toward a person of the opposite sex, he simply did nothing. Storms passed, he knew. Many a tempestuous sail was soothed by a wait. That was something every salty seafarer knew. But in this moment, all those nautical miles didn't matter. He was suddenly twelve years old again, longing for his first love. Life is funny in that way; you revisit experiences in some spiraling pattern. Desire, fear, anger; the only thing that changes is the number of age spots on your arm. And each time the experience arrives, you have a choice. You can say, "Yes," and act. You can say, "No," and act. Or you can do nothing and wait. Each choice has a course, and each course has a price. Mac chose.

He took a step away from her. The move helped to hide his nervousness. Besides, he felt he looked more sincere in perspective and discovered that a little distance helped. Then he turned back to her. "Do you want to get married?" Mac asked. Elizabeth tried to control her surprise, but it was too apparent on her face to hide. Mac felt sure that Elizabeth was not easily ruffled. He imagined that not much astounded her, but he snuck past her social preparedness and caught her unaware. "I know we only met," Mac went on, "and it is insane to even think of it but look at what we'd be gaining: You get a broken-down man with a broken-down yacht, and I get to save on sharing the royalties."

"One pound short and I file suit, marriage or no," Elizabeth joked.

"Does that mean you'd consider it?" Mac asked.

"Are you always a businessman?"

"Life is negotiation," he answered. That was true, she knew, at least her life was. Elizabeth's view of the world was realistic; that started early on. Maybe it was a result of being born of her working-class parents. Maybe it was that she was a woman. Or maybe it was because of her heritage. She was English. The English are a people known for stiff upper lips and not frenzied emotions. Lads at football games were the exception. Beer and bravado, with years of suppressed passion, birthed brawling. For the English, it wasn't acceptable to love a woman; only a football team.

Still, Elizabeth wanted something more. At least she thought she did. She didn't realize it. Not until she ran into Mac and his mad-as-a-hatter idea. But now?

"Do you have feelings for me?" she asked.

"Well, yes. I think I do."

"That's not exactly the response a woman who's just received a proposal hopes to hear," Elizabeth said with lifted eyebrows.

"Do you want me to tell you that I love you?" Mac asked.

"Do you?" Elizabeth queried in counter.

"We have a lot of fun. We laugh. We dance. You look good in a fountain. You think I'm charming. These are wonderful. But love? What is love? I've been married twice before, and I don't even know. I've been living on my boat now for twenty-five years. I've sailed through most of the world. The currents come and go. The wind changes. Even the tides shift daily. And still you sail on. That's the best that love can be. Twenty-five years on the sea. I am here. I have been living alone for many years. I am not lonely. There are always German tourists to drink with. And many others to amuse. And I enjoy my own company. I didn't even know I might feel otherwise until the other day. The conversation, the dancing, the kindness and graciousness you carry, I have not known a woman like you in a long time, and I am not prepared to live without the hope of having your company again. Is that love? I am not sure. But it seems like a good place to start. So, what do you say, do you want to marry me?"

Elizabeth looked at Mac. She had seen that look in his eyes before. Such sincerity. Such urgency. She believed what he said was true — for him — for now — for at least this moment. But would it be true for a week, a month, a decade? How would he change on cloudy days? What part of his declaration was solid enough to endure?

"Let me think about it," she said after a moment.

"Fair enough," Mac said, and then he embraced her with joy.

———

CHAPTER 29
The Photos

They arrived at Ernesto's, where the reveling was already underway. A trio played in the corner, and the local patrons were engaged in passionate conversation. Ernesto greeted them with relief.

"Where have you been?" he asked. "You didn't stop for lunch."

"My apologies," Mac bowed. "We got involved in what we were doing."

"That is completely understandable," the bar owner said, giving Elizabeth a wink.

"No," Mac said. "We were taking photographs."

"Be careful at customs," Ernesto said to Elizabeth. "T he officials will spend many hours looking at art." Elizabeth laughed.

"Not those kinds of photos," Mac said. "These are for our book. To put on the back cover and to send to the press." He took the camera from his pocket and opened a photo in the viewer. "Look, the fountain."

"Bellissima," Ernesto exclaimed. And it was; not only Elizabeth, but the photo was as well. The way the camera caught the glistening of the water, and the way the fountain showered the subject with joy. "So beautiful," Ernesto effused. Mac opened the next photo, one of Elizabeth and him. Ernesto made sounds of appreciation. "You are a handsome couple," Ernesto said.

"I said the same earlier," Mac affirmed.

They "oohed" and "aahed" through a dozen more frames, Elizabeth was as excited as Mac to share the afternoon fun like tourists after a scenic cruise. There they were. At the cathedral. At the table. With the children. In the costly jacket. Without the costly jacket. Playful, beckoning, engaging, surprising, inviting and exciting. That was what the photographs captured, and that was what Mac and Elizabeth felt. Each image increased the fun of the memory. And each memory magnified the joy of the moment. And so it went on, photo after photo, until the photo taken by the waiter that featured the trio at lunch, appeared on the screen.

"That's him," Ernesto said, pointing at the screen.

"That's the photographer we hired," Mac said.

"That is the man who was in here asking about you," Ernesto said. "The one I told you about yesterday. The investigator."

Mac thought his heart might explode.

* * * * * * * * *

Beth's cab ride to the airport was excruciating. Road construction made traffic unbearable. Beth found many things unbearable: Golf, lunch at the club, people who gossiped, people who complained about being busy, there was quite a list. Her marriage was one of them. David was a great guy. Everyone told her so. And she was happy that he was successful enough at work to provide the extras she wanted in an "a la carte" life, but was she happy? No. Her marriage was like the mess on the highway, constant negotiation. Even in the back seat of the taxi, she could feel the anxiety of driving as lanes closed, shifted, ended, and merged, each slowing the crawl of the stifling gas-guzzling, fume-emitting cars, buses, vans, trucks, and the infernal parade of SUVs. Dozens of SUVs. Hundreds of SUVs. Caravans of them. SUVs are suburbia's version of covered wagons, she decided. Pricey and pompous, they filled driveway after driveway, each riding higher and broader than the one before. Owners argued practicality and protection, but Beth knew the real purpose was status; ours is bigger; ours is shinier; ours has five automatic doors. Status, that was the reason for SUVs, at least for the semi-rich who haven't yet risen to the level of city pieds-a-terre or home helicopter ports. A helicopter might be fun, she thought, like an airborne limousine. She could fly from place to place, wearing noise-cancelling headphones and pouring wine into people's pools as she passed. Wouldn't that be fun? People would probably not even notice. If they thought there was a faint smell or a slight discoloration, they'd assume someone relieved themself while wading. That spoiled the fun for her. Why waste perfectly good wine if there wasn't even an annoyance factor? Well, with the windfall on the way, she could afford the wine she'd pour. How many pools could she pollute? Beth was wondering exactly how much money her father stashed away when the taxi driver screeched to a halt outside the airport terminal.

———

———

CHAPTER 30
Two Can Play

"Why is an investigator trying to find you?" Elizabeth asked when she and Mac moved outside the café. She'd kept her calm when the identification was made even though she was as startled as Mac was angry.

"That son of a bitch. I should have known something was up when he agreed to work so cheaply. And finding him, standing there on the promenade as if the world laid a treasure at my feet. He was waiting there for me. So he could follow me. And I played right into his hands, didn't I? Having him follow us around, taking photos and then paying him for the surveillance."

"Are you wanted by the law?" Elizabeth probed. "Did you embezzle money, romance the wrong woman?"

"No. Nothing like that," Mac said.

"But you are on the run?" Elizabeth pursued.

"Yes," Mac seethed, "from a rotten family."

"Your family?" Elizabeth wanted clarification.

"Heartless, self-serving blood-suckers," Mac incited. "We don't talk. We haven't once. Not one single time. Not since my first wife died."

"Do you mean your children?" she asked, trying to keep Mac on point.

"Yes. Three of them. First wife. I was young," Mac defended.

"You didn't say." Elizabeth was only somewhat concerned. After all, they'd only just met. She couldn't expect to know everything about a person in a few hours. But still, why would a man omit an important detail like this?

"Well," Mac continued, "they are not children anymore. Offspring. Thorns of my loins."

"And they hired this investigator?" Elizabeth wanted to know.

"That's what Ernesto said Dennis told him."

"So, you knew?" Elizabeth asked.

He didn't want to believe it. He didn't want to know. Now Mac huffed in resigned anger and replied, "Suspected."

Elizabeth allowed a quiet moment to pass before she spoke again. "Why? What did you do?" she asked.

"Nothing. I didn't do anything. I left. My wife and me. We didn't just run off. There was money. They didn't starve. They were adults. They weren't abandoned."

"Then why did they send a man to find you?" Elizabeth asked.

"I don't know, but I will find out. I'll go talk to Dennis. After I beat the shit out of him."

"Mac, don't do anything you'll regret," Elizabeth advised.

Regret? He wanted to laugh. Regret being a salesman? Regret marrying a conniving woman? Regret having sex that resulted in children and taking on the duty and obligations that come with a family? What would there be to remember of his earlier life if there was no regret? He looked at Elizabeth quietly for another moment before he spoke. "It's too late to worry about that. But it is not too late to find out what is going on." He took her arm and started to move them in the direction of the square. Elizabeth stopped him.

"How will you find Dennis?" she asked. "Do you know where he is staying? Do you have a phone number, a business card? Do you even know if he gave his real name?"

"He gave me a card," Mac defended, "but I don't know if any of the information is true, and I did not ask where he was staying in Palma." Mac felt swindled, naïve, and foolish. "I will call the number on his card from a pay phone and see if he picks up, but even if he does, I don't know if he'll tell me where he is, considering he is a liar and a con man. But," Mac said, holding up his camera, "I have his photo. Two people can play this game."

––––––––––––

———————

CHAPTER 31
Beth and Time

Beth calculated that Michael was almost twelve hours ahead of her. With a ten-hour travel time to Majorca, she would have to deplane and hunt them down like a foxhound. Still, Palma might be massive, and there was no certainty that they'd leave a strong scent. She remembered her father's penchant for cheap wine, and she could smell a bad bouquet from a block away, but she didn't think that would be enough to find those rotten bastards. She needed some way to trim the scope.

She might look for harbors where her father could anchor, but she wasn't sure after all these years that she'd recognize Noah's ark, and she didn't want to spend her time hunting down the mythical Flying Dutchman. That is awfully à propos she chuckled to herself. Father on a ship, unable to make port, and doomed to sail forever on the sea. That was him, wasn't it? What was the story? Lost off the Cape of Good Hope? Floundering in a thick dark cloud? Looking for a faithful woman who would love him and end his sea-captive journey? What was her name? Oh yes, Pandora. No, Senta. Whichever, it is all the same, Beth mused. Another hopeless man, another joyless love, and another sailor who would never come home.

Armed with a boarding pass and a light carry-on with undies, Beth made her way to the appointed gate just as the flight was being announced. That suited her. She hated to wait. Not for a taxi, not for a plane, and not for her father's love.

Maybe the best strategy, when she got to the island, was to find Michael and force him to take her to their father. It would have to be easier to find her brother. She knew his name. She knew he'd be in a hotel. All she needed to do was find the right hotel. Still, that could take hours that she didn't have.

In those last few moments before she boarded, she had an inspiration and called her brother's secretary at his office. "Oh, hello, Susie," she cooed into the phone. "This is Michael's sister, Beth. You will never believe this. I am on my way to meet Michael in Majorca, and I forgot to bring the note I'd written with the name of the hotel. I was considering running around the island shouting for him, but could you be a dear and tell me where he is staying?"

The secretary capitulated without fuss and turned over the name of the hotel. Beth had her trained. Beth could be obnoxious to service workers who did not immediately do what she asked. Once, several years ago, Beth made a similar request about an insurance firm that Michael used. Susie said she wasn't sure she could give her the name of the company. Beth screamed and hollered and played the snooty, rich, sister-of-your-boss card, following up her performance with a sharp, if untrue, retelling of the conversation to Michael. After Beth raged on and on until his head ached, Michael told his secretary to just give her the information she wanted. Beth could be a bitch. It took her years to perfect the skill. Now she thanked Susie profusely for once again "saving the day" and asked questions about Susie's mother, as if she cared. Susie gave Beth simple answers in a good-natured and grateful voice. The secretary could have elaborated on the condition of her mother's illnesses, which absorbed most of her free time, but there was no point in sharing your troubles with someone who was really only concerned about herself, so she didn't.

With the information she wanted, Beth clicked off and sat for a moment with her phone poised. Thankfully she had booked a hotel on the opposite side of the city from the one Michael would be in. That gave her the advantage of surprise. She smiled at the idea of catching Michael off guard. Then she hit a number on her list of contacts.

———————

CHAPTER 32
The Third Leg of the Triangle

After several rings, in what seemed to Beth an interminable time, a voice answered, "Hello?"

"Hello, Jonathan," Beth said moderately. There was silence on the phone, no immediate response. Beth continued. "It's your sister."

"I know who it is," Jonathan returned in caution.

Beth could not remember exactly when she and her brother became so tentative with each other. Jonathan was the youngest, and she supposed that was part of it. While Michael felt the burden of being the oldest son and assumed the responsibility of being the family pacifier, Jonathan stepped back. He was the watcher. He watched from a carefully guarded place. Maybe it was for protection, Beth thought. A way to stay out of the drama. There was enough family drama with her father's bad behavior, and the unsettled relationship between her parents, and the boat, and the sailing, and the cheating, and the illness, and . . . oh, how the list went on. Do all families have these sorts of stories, Beth wondered? She thought of the tales she heard at lunches when drinks pried secrets from the women she knew. She didn't use the word friends. Friends usually think kindly of each other. These women did not.

"Have you heard from Michael?" Beth asked her younger brother.

Jonathan was slow to answer. He wondered why his sister was asking. Finally, he said, "Yes, a few weeks ago."

Jonathan's hesitation intrigued Beth. "Oh, then he told you what he was up to?" Beth asked.

"The usual," Jonathan replied.

"Did he tell you he was going to Majorca?"

"No, he didn't mention it. On a vacation? I understand it is beautiful there. Great sun."

"He isn't going for the weather," Beth offered.

Jonathan was quiet. He knew his sister well. She never called to just say hello or to ask about his health. She always wanted something. And he knew how she operated. She'd throw out little bits and pieces, like bait, and wait for you to bite. Then she'd bite back. In time he learned that silence was useful. He learned that years ago, and not just with his sister.

"Did you hear me?" Beth summoned. "Michael is going to Majorca to visit Father."

Thousands of thoughts exploded in Jonathan's mind. What? Where? How? Father in Majorca? What was he doing there? Why was Michael going to visit? Was Beth making this up? He couldn't always be sure that the things she said were fact. She had a way, not exactly of fabricating things, or imagining them, but of seeing things from such an odd perspective that she may report what she believed was true, even when it sometimes wasn't. Jonathan considered what to say. He didn't want to play into her game, whatever it was. That never went well. Being confused or stupefied led to slippery slopes. He didn't want to express surprise, though he was.

"I'm sure they'll have a wonderful visit," Jonathan said with as much simplicity as he could.

Now, Beth bit. "A wonderful visit? That is the most non-committal comment I've ever heard. Aren't you surprised? Curious? Bewildered? Puzzled? Mystified?"

"I didn't know Father was in Spain," Jonathan said.

"None of us did," Beth raged. "Not a word, not a phone call, not a postcard. Nothing. Not since Mother died."

"It was a difficult time for him," Jonathan offered.

"For him?" she screeched. "What are you talking about? Mother's death meant nothing to Father. He dumped her before she even became ill, remember? He'd moved on and left her. As far as our father was concerned, Mother died when he took up with that Brit bitch, a long time before she passed." Beth sounded as if she was shaking with contempt. She was slow to heal, Jonathan knew. A scratch, a bump, or a bruise took his sister twice as long to recover from as any normal person. It was almost as if she held onto the boo-boo so she could show the wound to all. That had always irritated Jonathan. She'd make such a scene that she stole all the attention from her brothers.

Michael was the mature one; he deferred to Beth's drama addiction. But Jonathan had no choice in that dynamic. He was shoved out of the nurturing by the sheer power of her histrionics. He never felt it was fair, but he learned early on that expecting fairness was a path to disappointment, especially where it concerned Beth.

"I'm not standing up for Father," Jonathan assured, "but there is always more to a situation than any one person can see."

"Oh, for Christ's sake. Are you taking a continuing education course in psychology at the community college?" Beth taunted.

Jonathan knew that the strongest action was no retort. He knew that his sister was deaf to consideration and reason, but he decided not to take heed of this knowledge. Instead, he said, "Beth, you are self-absorbed."

"And why shouldn't I be, Jonathan? Why shouldn't I be?" Beth asked indignantly. "Who would be there to watch out for me if not myself? Michael? My husband, David? You? It was never Father. Do you want me to tell you why Michael is going to Majorca? Would it surprise you to know that he is not going for the beach?"

There was the pause he was waiting for, the dramatic pause, the card-playing pause, the pause of power. It was always a part of the conversation with his sister. She'd wait. He'd wait. Tactical silence stretched between them like a sharp wire. Why couldn't communication be easy? For him, for them, for his family? Jonathan had watched this tug of war all throughout his childhood and young adult life. The stinging remark or the pointed question had set the tone for the tension. The payoff was never a warm embrace, but a cold attack. That was what he saw in his family. It was one of the things that kept him distanced. Intimacy is a weakness when emotions are bartered, and secrets are currency. Beth's bruises were always displayed, but Jonathan had a history of them as well. Only he kept them quiet. He watched and tried to remain unattached despite the bidding war that went on for his alliance. He didn't understand. Why would anyone go through such an effort when forthrightness was so simple? Did being devious and circumspect add more to the rightness of the truth? Why did so much of his family dynamic involve trying to buy support? He didn't want to take sides. He didn't want to fight. He wanted life to move forward with unity and happiness. He was born into the wrong family for that, he often thought. So, he didn't take sides. He didn't choose. He watched, and he waited. And he hoped. He hoped they would just leave him out of it. He hoped they'd stop trying to recruit him.

Finally, as he knew she would, Beth could not stand the silence any longer. She revealed the trump card. "Father has a stash of cash."

"I'm sure he does," Jonathan chose as his response.

"A lot, I bet," Beth fueled.

"So?" Jonathan asked.

"Michael is going there to get it," Beth played. "Michael is going there to see Father, squeeze the money from him, and cut you and me out."

"Isn't that between Michael and Father?" Jonathan queried.

"That money belongs to all of us," Beth insisted. "We are the family."

"The money belongs to Father, doesn't it?"

"That is something the courts can decide," Beth ridiculed, "unless you've been studying law now."

"Why would you think the money isn't his?" Jonathan asked.

"Well, if it was accumulated when Mother was still alive, say before the divorce, then it would be an asset he didn't identify, and half would be a part of Mother's estate. Since we're the beneficiaries of her holdings, a part of that money would belong to us by right." Beth did not make an audible sound, but Jonathan could hear the triumph in her stillness.

"That is why Michael is going," she went on. "He wants to confront the embezzler and collect the prize. Our brother likely found discrepancies in papers, or maybe that woman Father has as a business manager said something, and Michael realized there was a stash. Maybe it's under the floorboards of that rickety old boat. And Michael doesn't intend on leaving it sit." There, Beth had laid it out.

Jonathan was suddenly suspicious. "Where are you calling from?" he asked.

"Does it matter?" asked Beth.

"You're at the airport, aren't you?" Jonathan pried.

"Well, you don't expect me to sit idly by while Michael takes everything, do you?"

"So, why did you call? What do you want from me?"

"Two are better than one to stop a thief. Three are better than two to extort a run-away parent," Beth posed. "It could be a lot of money. It must be, for Michael to notice. Don't you want your share?"

As the youngest sibling and as the one most in the shadows, Jonathan lived a life out of the battle. He kept his sanity by standing apart from the exploding bombs and out of the reach of the lacerating daggers. He always watched as Mother tried to push Father into the oncoming path, even when she wielded the weapons. He watched as Michael tried to defuse the torpedoes one by one before they hit. And he watched as Beth escalated the situation by playing dress-up with emotions. Jonathan was always on the sidelines, watching, waiting, ready to turn, and run.

He remembered the night, the family-changing night. To say it was where it all began was simplistic. The fault lines were in place for many years before the earth quaked. Given all the aspirations and expectations of his family, the tectonic shift was more a matter of when than if. After the initial screaming, the family shushed and hushed, all trying to be quiet. They insisted they should leave Jonathan out of it. They said he was in bed, sleeping soundly, and did not hear anything, but that was not true. He was in the shadows in the hall that opened to the doorway. He could not see into the room, so he did not see everything, but he saw them, his brother and his mother, watching in shock. He saw the horror on their faces, the judgmental accusations, the rage, and he knew that even in its disheveled pretend state, his family would never be the same. And when the lights came on, instead of walking into the room to be a part of the melee, Jonathan peeked quietly around the corner and then returned to bed without a word.

"So, Brother, do you want to fly to Majorca and help me? Do you want what is owed to you?" Beth brought it home.

There was a moment of silence, then Jonathan said, "No."

"Wait," Beth said astonished. "Are you saying you don't want your share?"

"Yes," said Jonathan, "I don't want anything. I have plenty. There is nothing I need. Whatever is going on, just leave me out of it."

Beth could not believe what she was hearing. "You," she said, "you are just like Father. Never wanting to be involved. Never wanting to be a part of this family. Well, don't come begging for it later," she told Jonathan. "You won't get any." Then she disconnected angrily.

Jonathan shook his head. Sometimes, he thought, it's best to not be involved. Not when the fight was so nasty and the price so great. What could he need that was worth that? Then he took a moment and pressed buttons on his cell phone, blocking his sister's number. At least for now, he thought, at least until she settles down.

Jonathan's partner, Robert, put his head into the study. "Who was that?" he asked.

"No one, really. My sister," Jonathan said.

Robert looked up at the ceiling with "doesn't-she-ever-rest" eyes and then crossed to Jonathan. "She's like a rash," Robert commented.

"Yes, persistent and irritating. I blocked her calls," Jonathan reported.

"Good." He kissed Jonathan on the cheek and walked out of the room.

Jonathan lived through enough drama. He didn't want more. The best thing he could do was to put it out of his mind and go back to the work he was doing. And that is what he did.

————

CHAPTER 33
The Search

Mac escorted Elizabeth back to her hotel, trying to soothe the jangle with assurances that there was nothing to be concerned about. Elizabeth wanted to believe him, but she couldn't escape the anxiety that washed over her. Mac was mad. So was she. But she was not the object of the investigator's hunt. She was angry on her own. She was angry because Mac withheld information that his past was possibly present. Children? Investigators? And to be going on for several days? She could understand how Mac could be concerned about revealing his history to her, but the discovery of an embittered family conflict is not a strong trust-builder. Mac promised to visit her in the morning with a report. "And we can talk about the future," he said. "Unless you want to say 'No,' right now."

"Of course not," Elizabeth said.

"I would understand," Mac said. "It is never good to find out too much about a person," Mac said. "People are easier to like if you don't see them from all sides."

"Everyone has a past," Elizabeth said realistically. "Just maybe not as colorful," she added. "Now go. Find out what you need to know. We can sort out everything tomorrow." Then they shared a quick kiss on the cheek and parted — Elizabeth into the hotel lobby, and Mac into the night.

Well, this was an interesting turn of events, Elizabeth thought, as she made her way to her hotel room. Secrets. Lots of secrets. Secrets open doors for possibilities. She worked in an insurance firm. She was used to weighing possibilities. Good ones and bad ones. She would have to spend some time examining these.

Mac sped off in search of the dissembling investigator. He stopped at the nearest phone station and dialed the number on the card. When the call went to an automated voice message, Mac hung up in anger. Stupid, stupid, stupid, Mac thought. That's what you get for believing in someone. It would be simple to chalk this up to one more life disappointment, but Mac wasn't giving up. He would find the trickster. He would show the photo around, and he'd find him. There were hotels to search, restaurants, and the camera shop. The clerks at the shop would remember the photographer. Mac would go there first. But it was late, and the shop would be closed, so he'd have to wait till tomorrow. But he didn't want to wait. He'd start with hotels. Still, there were dozens of hotels in Palma, ranging from modest to luxurious. The lying photographer could be in any of them. It would take hours. How could he not have found out where the guy with the camera was staying, Mac thought? How could he think the man was a gift from the fates? Mac was so swept up in the excitement, the anticipation of success, that he forgot to plan for surprises.

He stopped at six hotels on his way across town, without result. He would work his way toward the dock where he first met the photographer. Someone would remember his camera, if not his face. But workers change with shifts, and night clerks are not the same people as the ones who manned the earlier hours, so his canvasing bore no positive results. With each stop that brought a negative reply, Mac grew angrier. He felt more betrayed and more threatened. He let his guard down. His years in Majorca made him less suspicious, less astute. There was a time when he could tell a fraud from a mile away. He knew when someone was not telling the truth. He trusted his instincts, and they always brought him through safely. But not this time. This time, he was duped. This time, he was deceived. After two hours of front-clerk interviews, Mac decided to give up and return to his boat. A little rest would give him time to think over the situation. He staggered along the waterfront toward the ramp to his dinghy and then heard the voice from beyond the streetlight glow.

"Mac." Mac turned with surprise that changed to rage when he saw the investigator sitting on Mac's bench. The betrayed man walked aggressively toward the seated photographer.

"You bastard," Mac shouted, and he lurched toward Dennis with ready hands. Dennis responded with a quickness and skill that must be needed for investigation work. He rose, sidestepped Mac, and fended off the advancing fists. They struggled for a moment, then Dennis restrained the flailing anger, let the balloon deflate, and eased Mac onto the bay-front bench.

"Who are you?" Mac demanded, catching his breath.

"I knew it was a mistake to allow you to take the photograph," Dennis conceded. "Did the bar owner ID me?"

"He has a memory for faces, especially those of disreputable visitors asking questions. That's why you didn't go with us tonight."

"It was a consideration," the investigator acknowledged. "I thought it would be better not to take the risk."

"Who hired you? Who sent you to Majorca?" Mac wanted to know.

Dennis was silent for a moment. He never agreed to client confidentiality. It wasn't a part of the discussion. This was not an ethical dilemma; this was a personal one. What pain would the disclosure cause? What wound could silence avoid? Would it be worse if Mac knew? Isn't there compassion in not telling? Maybe there is more compassion in revealing. Dennis finally spoke. "Your son, Michael."

Mac stared at him for a moment, trying to grasp what Dennis said. Then Mac asked, "Why?"

"I don't know. He hired me to find you. That's all."

"So, you pretended to be a photographer?"

"I am a photographer. I take photographs all the time. It's just not my primary occupation. Don't forget, I was standing on the dock. You approached me. I told you it was a hobby. I never misrepresented myself," Dennis outlined.

"I feel betrayed. I feel conned. You were so engaging today. It was fun. I let myself be open. I extended my friendship to you. And then to find this out. It's like having a date with a woman who turns out to be a prostitute, one who pretends to like you and then asks you to pay." Mac thought they were having fun. Mac invited the man to join them at Ernesto's because he liked the man's company. Mac released an angry sigh and then said, "I thought you cared."

"Caring is an occupational hazard," Dennis said. "It is one I try to avoid. But I wasn't hardened enough. I have been sitting here, waiting for two hours. Waiting for you to come by on your way home. You and Elizabeth were kind to me today. Treating a total stranger like a pal. It meant a lot to me. The generosity. The acceptance. Watching from a distance, you never feel you are a part of things. You invited me in. That was nice."

"So, you came to say thank you? Well, fuck you."

"Yeah, fuck me," Dennis said and sat down. What a shit job, Dennis thought. He felt like a cop arresting a family friend's kid, or a tax collector foreclosing on a penniless widow. He was just as bad. He was a private investigator, chasing a likable old man on a magical island. What part of what was to come was his responsibility? The son could mean well, but if he didn't, and this man's life was somehow lessened, could Dennis forgive himself?

Mac sat on the bench, bereft of anger, and looked for an action that would turn the damage to a positive, or at least quarantine the effect. He turned to Dennis. "What would it take to forget the whole thing?" Mac asked quietly. "Just tell my son you couldn't find me."

"It is too late for that," Dennis said with regret. "I spoke with him yesterday to confirm it was you."

"Then why did you come here?" Mac asked.

"I came to tell you that your son will arrive in the morning at eight. I meet with him at the airport before I fly home."

———

––––––––––

CHAPTER 34
Sleepless Night

A red-eye flight is one of the most horrific ways to travel. Even if you manage to sleep, your biorhythms are smarter than alarm clocks and know perfectly well that when you wake to greet the sun, you should be putting yourself into comfy pajamas and meeting a mattress for a good sleep. Beth cursed her brother as the plane sailed off across the ocean. If Michael wasn't so sneaky and greedy, the entire excursion could have been planned, and her father's shakedown might have served the dual purpose of a much needed and exotic getaway. She would have to remember to take the airfare from Michael's share of the profits. He could write it off as a business expense. He was good at those sorts of things. He discovered the stashed cash, didn't he? She seriously doubted that her father, in an act of remorse, telegraphed Michael to confess.

She wouldn't be surprised if her father actually stowed the assets under the floor of the cabin of that ridiculous boat. That was probably why the old man built it himself; to make the secret hold. How much space does it take to hide a fortune? Two square feet? Eight? It depends on the denominations, she thought, and how much the total was. It must be a pretty hefty amount, or Michael wouldn't waste his time. A million? Maybe it was two million. If she got half . . . What would she do with a million dollars?

First, she'd file for divorce. She surely could find some evidence to force her husband's compliance. No one is sinless. She could uncover something. And if not, she'd make something up. It's amazing how far she could get with a weepy eye and a simple lie. And if he contested, even better. She'd take half of everything, for now and forever. She'd buy herself a she-pad and a handsome young guy with tight skin and a butt built for bouncing quarters.

Life with her husband wasn't bad. It was just that it was David. No spark, no sizzle, no excitement, just David. It was that good, old, steady, sturdy, sincere sameness day after day that drove her to drink. What she needed now was a little sleep. She took the pillbox from her handbag and fished out a sleeping aid. Thankfully, there was a prescription on call with the doctor. One of these and a stiff drink or two and she would land in Majorca, rested and ready. She reached up and pulled the flight-attendant call button. Now, what was she thinking about? Oh yes, her husband.

When she first met her husband, she was grateful for his dullness. Children are attracted to people who have a character opposite from their parents. A daughter with a good-boy father is drawn to a bad-guy boyfriend. A disreputable father leads to a boring husband.

Being with David was so safe, so soothing, after the life she and her siblings endured with her father — crazy, drunk, all that chatter, those countless unfunny jokes — and then his — what he did — how could he? The flight attendant arrived at her seat, interrupting her thoughts. "How can I help you, ma'am?" the attendant asked.

"Well, you can respond a little more quickly," Beth sniped.

"Is there something you need?" the attendant asked coolly.

"Yes. A gin and tonic. Two. With lemon, not lime. And before we reach Spain, please." The attendant smiled a "f-you" smile and tottered down the aisle. "Bitch," Beth said under her breath.

* * * * * * * * *

Airborne Beth, in her barbiturate subdued bitchiness, was the only one in this menagerie destined for sleep that night.

Elizabeth Kensington, nee Schoenhauer, spent most of the late hours pacing, wearing a trench in her hotel room floor, trying to figure out what could have possibly happened with Mac's children. She conjured up many scenarios, each more entangled than the one before. She suspected none would come near to matching the truth. The only thing more complicated than imagination is reality.

Why would Mac's son send an investigator to find him? How could his son not know where his father was? Didn't they talk or write? A postcard with a quick line? Did his son think his father was dead? What happened between them? How long were they estranged? A year, two, many? During that time, was there no overture to bridge the gap? Wouldn't time normally repair a fissure? A hurt of the heart heals slowly, she knew, but it can mend.

And why did Mac behave the way he did? It was something she was not prepared to witness. His otherwise forthright and charismatic nature turned to rage. Blistering-hot fury. Anger so raw she could feel it through space. Was it because he was deceived by a photographer transformed, a presumed cohort unmasked as a finder of runaways? Did he feel betrayed by a stranger? Or was it because his invented life was interrupted?

She knew little of Mac's past. She knew of the wives, and the death, and the escape, and the plan to fool the world of book publishers. But she didn't speculate on more detail. And that was not normal for her. She often thought her emotional survival came from the anticipation of exposure and the preparation for the surprising side of people. She never allowed herself to lower her walls. But here, she was not alert. With Mac, she set aside her common sense to be suspicious.

She found him charming and daring. He would get such glee from pulling off the hoax he planned. It would be a great revelation to make at parties and dinners, the story of how he'd hoodwinked them all. She thought it was fun too. She never gave a good look at what might drive such a complex scheme. She never considered why Mac would want to pretend. A con man might plan a charade to hook a mark into a financial investment. A promise of return and then a disappearance, followed by disappointment. She did not think that was Mac's mission. Maybe he wanted to hide cash or displace assets. But why go through such extremes? Maybe it was something simpler. Maybe he was hoping to cover up the glimmer of insight that he might not be any good as a writer.

That would explain the look, the uneasiness she saw. And then proposing? Why did he propose? Did he really have feelings for her? Did he hope to cement her impersonation as the mysterious author? Was he afraid she would reveal the truth? Did he think that a proposal would anchor the illusion? Did he believe that somehow, he would be more of what he wanted to be if she said yes? Maybe what she saw in his face was fear.

* * * * * * * * *

Ernesto divided the world into three parts: His family and friends, the people who lived in Majorca, and everyone else. It helped him to prioritize his worrying. Mac had been floating around Palma for so long, he'd moved into the inner circle of concern. Ernesto watched Mac slip in and out of love with one trollop or another and concoct more plans for fame than anyone could dream up. The two men shared insights, commiserated sins, celebrated the days, and bonded as friends.

It was a great confusion for Ernesto when he saw the investigator in the photograph on Mac's camera. He already told his friend of the inquiry. But discovering that the man managed such a close-range association took him by surprise. Whatever storm was coming, it was on the immediate horizon, and whether it was a simple thunderstorm or a massive hurricane, Ernesto knew being prepared was always best.

When he saw the man in the photograph, he first considered not saying anything. But who knows what might have happened? And if something did, and he was silent, how would he feel? He made the identification because he wanted his friend to have a chance to brace himself before the gale hit. To hide, to run, to escape, to find shelter, or to prepare for whatever was heading his way. Knowing that he did the right thing did not prevent him from worrying. Inner circles are tricky. It is much easier not to care.

* * * * * * * * *

Dennis returned to his hotel feeling like a sleazebag. He felt guilty since the lunch during the photographic shooting session. He thought he was so clever to agree to act as the photographer for the very man he was there to spy on. It was almost genius. He never suspected he would get swept up in the carefree comradery.

Earlier that evening, the faux friend decided to come clean with Mac. His trip dockside was a "no harm, no foul" effort to wash his guilt out to sea. But when he discovered he was found out; he knew all would not be forgiven. He stepped on the open hand the old man extended. And the confession that might have whitewashed the culpability of his ruse, instead, landed him, as he deserved to be, at the center of thoughtless transgression.

He packed his things, except his travel bath kit, poured himself a scotch, and waited for the fog that would shield him from self-recrimination until the alarm rang. In the morning, he would rise to step away from this chapter. Except . . . except . . . he wished he'd have other chances to prove himself a worthy friend.

* * * * * * * *

Mac was not a worrier. Once or twice when waves were wrathful, and his tiny home struggled to remain above water, he wondered if he and the boat would make it through the storm safe and sound. Knowing there was nothing he could do but tie himself to the rail and wait, he'd abandoned hope. If they sank, he may drown. If they floated, he may die in the sea, and so he decided there was no point in worry. He sang instead and watched the water rise in walls and encompass him.

In most incidents, Mac was a planner. Action was the key in almost every situation. In the past, when faced with an oncoming collision, he thought through the results of each maneuver, and then he'd choose accordingly.

He thought of moving the boat. He could run down the coast and find some cove or dock and hide. But there was Elizabeth. He didn't want her to think he was running away from her. He could go to her hotel and ask her to go with him, but he wasn't sure he wanted to place her in a position to make a choice that did not include him in her future.

And if he sailed away, what would prevent them from finding him again? They located him even after all this time and with all the world to disappear into. It would be easy to track him down in nearby waters.

He wasn't frightened by the idea of seeing his son. He was affronted. It was so like his children to insist that they have what they want, regardless of the discomfort it would cause him. They were all that way, all three of them, in varying degrees of self-centeredness. And what could his son want? Money? Perhaps there was a death? Maybe he wanted to revisit his anger over the loss of his mother? Or to remind his father of how he abandoned them? Or the pain he caused when he separated from his wife? How he caused her death? Or those accusations his daughter made?

Mac could add another half-dozen possibilities to the list, but speculation was of little value. Instead, he decided what he would do. In the morning, he would wait. He would work on the boat and wait. And if his son was aggressive or belligerent, he would use the flare gun to force Michael to jump overboard and swim back to shore.

* * * * * * * *

High above the Mediterranean, the silence of sleeping passengers was invaded by a gasping scream. Michael bolted upright in a sweat. He was disoriented, and it took a moment for him to remember where he was. Two flight attendants appeared by his seat.

"Are you all right?" one asked.

"Yes. I . . . I . . . It was a dream. A bad dream."

"Do you need anything? Some water?" asked the other attendant.

"Yes. Water, thank you." One attendant moved down the aisle to the kitchen. "It was strange," said Michael. "I don't dream. Nothing I remember. They say we dream, all the time, but I can't attest to it. I can remember getting up in the night to get a drink of water or use the bathroom, but if I was dreaming, I don't know what the dreams were."

The flight attendant, who went to the galley, returned with a bottle of water. Michael unscrewed the cap and drank eagerly. "Are you feeling better?" the attendant asked. "Do you need medical attention?"

"No," Michael said, visibly calmer. "I'm fine. Really. I was startled, that's all."

"It happens all the time," the attendant said. "Especially on these long red-eye flights. People get excited or anxious, and it comes out when they nap."

"Yes." Michael said. "Thank you."

"Just use the call button if you need anything," the attendant said.

"Thank you." And then the attendants walked away, leaving Michael to replay the memory of his dream. In it, he saw his father, standing on a beach, at least Michael thought it was a beach, and when Michael walked toward his father, he realized his father was screaming and burning on fire.

———

CHAPTER 35
The Sunrise in Majorca

There is nothing as beautiful as the morning in Majorca. Mac thought that every day since he arrived in this haven of wonder. The beautiful clear sky, the inviting azure water, and the surrounding magnificent vista filled him with peace. Filled him with possibilities. But today something was off. The blue of the sky was less vivid. There was a grayish hue to the water of the bay. And the sunlight that streaked the town with its usual golden promise looked harsh and unrelenting. Damn it, thought Mac, they've done it again. So many years of freedom, after a life of servitude, and these children managed to send the tentacles of the past to leach the joy from the morning.

He never really wanted children. That was his wife's passion. She liked taking care of things, arranging them to be just so. That's what she did with the children. She dressed them, arranged them, and cared for them, using her love to create allies. She turned them into soldiers of her one-woman empire. He was left to work, earn, plan, save, and provide no matter what level of expense was needed to create the image of the family she wanted. And he was good at it. Clever, inventive, tireless at first, driven by her increasing demand for the picture-perfect life — until that day.

He fought with depression for at least a decade. He did not understand why he felt listless and detached. In the beginning of the

149

marriage, he was the center. He was the celebration. He was the love. Before. Then he was the extra wheel. The breadwinner. He was an auxiliary guest at a party that used to be for him. That was when he realized that his life wasn't the life he wanted. When he did, he started to escape. At first, he worked late, avoiding home. Then he started drinking a little, not excessively, at least not often, but more and more until that horrible night.

Sex was one of his favorite exercises. His wife was beautiful, and everyone thought they were a perfect partnership. Maybe they were in the beginning. He remembered romance and companionship, a courting that lasted long after the wedding. And sex. Regular sex. Plenty of sex with passion and gusto, praise for delight. It was only after the family started to expand that he began to realize that his wife used the intimacy to barter — like a treat on a good day — doling it out to keep the provider on the path, to keep the worker on track, to keep the money coming in.

That is when the tide turned, with that first realization of cruelty. The understanding that the freely given affection was not free but calculated. And as the children multiplied, the ration was further divided. He wasn't the first, the main, or the central target of those eyes and smile, of the laughter and praise, but the second, then the third, and then obscure. That's when the depression started. That's when he began drinking, finding companionship with bartenders, clients, or regulars at the places he frequented, united as they were by the commonality of a disgruntled existence. Alcohol is oil for an unhappy machine.

The difficulty is that alcohol creates a fog of consciousness. Most things look better when viewed in a haze. Distortion creates its own prism of reality, and in that world, actions have imagined consequences only, and memory isn't real, but a collected subjectiveness.

That was the night. Intoxicated and fueled by martini perception, he came home with a desire for action, for physical pleasure, not necessarily sex, but some way to feel connected, to feel loved. He wanted just to touch life again.

He stumbled into the family room, knocking a piece of bric-à-brac from the table, and he most likely would have fallen but for the steadying hand that reached out to keep him keeled. Encouraged by the caring, he embraced the giver in eager and tender need.

He was warmed, at least in his memory, by the fondness of the steadying hand. He translated that fondness to desire, and he moved his hands across the pliant body, kissed his wife, and reached his hands to cup those lovely breasts he hungered for. He heard the gasp, almost surprise, as he slid his hand down to the place between her legs that for so long was a place of pleasure. The scream, followed by the harsh overhead light, pulled him from his ecstasy. From the doorway, his wife looked at him in shock. His oldest son stood in her shadow. The girl in his arms, screaming and moving away, was his daughter.

———————

CHAPTER 36
At the Terminal Meeting

Dennis arrived early at the airport. The first flights of the day were often ahead of schedule as airlines hoped to accommodate for time-consuming surprises.

Having learned the art of traveling lightly, he carted only his carry-on and camera bag as he checked the arrival-departure screen and headed to the listed gate to wait. To a casual observer, he looked like a tourist heading home from a holiday.

At ten till eight, the arriving plane touched tarmac and taxied to the gate. After landing procedures, the gate agent opened the door, and arriving passengers made their way into the terminal. Michael was easy to spot. He was obviously not a long-distance traveler. He carried a sports jacket over his arm and looked weary and disquieted.

"How was the flight? Dennis asked.

"Long," Michael replied.

No chit chat, Dennis thought. That was all right. He never got the impression that this client was best friend material. He was concise and expected results. Dennis delivered.

"Where is he?" Michael asked.

"His boat is harbored at the south end of the bay," Dennis reported. Michael nodded. They walked for a few yards, and then Dennis asked, "What are your plans?"

"First the hotel and a chance to wash away the flight. And then — find my father."

"He sometimes has breakfast at a local café, but I think he'll be on the boat this morning. He knows you're coming."

"How?"

"A local bar owner identified me from when I was asking around," Dennis replied simply.

"We agreed on discretion."

"I was discrete, not invisible."

Michael looked annoyed. "He didn't run off, did he? Sail away?"

Dennis wondered the same. How would Mac deal with the news? Would he wait for a warm-hearted embrace or pull anchor and disappear with his ship like love on a cloudy day? To be certain, Dennis stopped at the harbor to see before heading to the airport. "The boat was there this morning. I checked on my way here," Dennis reported to Michael.

"Well, no harm. If he knows, he knows. He would have known soon enough. I don't think his knowing makes any difference. It may be better. I wouldn't want him to have a stroke."

"Why do you want him?" Dennis asked. That question was on his mind since the day he met Mac. "Why did you hire me to find him?"

"Does it matter?" Michael asked.

"No, I wondered, that's all," Dennis replied.

"He got to you, didn't he," Michael said. "He pulled you in with that salesman's bullshit." Dennis was startled for a moment but hid behind his professional mask. "I can see it in your eyes," Michael said. "He scams everyone. That best friend confidentiality, the easy-going banter. The man can talk you into anything. He just keeps going, pouring it on, till you find yourself swept up in the tidal wave. Enchanted. Mesmerized. Sometimes agreeing to his latest scheme just to get him to shut up. He is so benevolent, so big-hearted, so clever. I've seen it a million times. Don't feel bad; he fools everyone. They all get involved, get their hopes up, over and over again, but in the end, he never delivers. It's all for him and nothing for anyone else. I don't mean to sound harsh. But once you peek behind the facade, it's easy to see."

Dennis nodded. "There is something irrepressible in his insistence to make life more than it is."

"Ha," Michael chortled. "Hook, line and sinker."

"I like him," Dennis said. "BS or not, I like him. Please be gentle." Then he picked up his travel bag and walked into the terminal.

———

———————

CHAPTER 37
Three Hours till Land

Beth, still roaring through the sky, heard the snoring long before her eyes opened and was surprised to realize that the menacing sound of a swooping bomber plane was coming from her. After two gin and tonics, she took her sleeping medication, one of the expensive kind, and slumbered off into La La Land for the duration of her time in the air. It was such a practical way to cross the sea, she thought. Scrap the in-flight films and leave the latest biography on your nightstand to serve the function for which it was intended — to avoid bed-time intimacy. She would spend the remainder of the travel time, drifting cozily in a rejuvenating state and then rise with the day ready for battle. At least that was the theory. Only she didn't feel rested. She didn't feel refreshed. She was foggy and frizzy and filmy and filthy. She smelled coffee and thought salvation was at hand, but even the gourmet blend and reasonably fresh croissant with Gruyere did not do the trick. She felt hung-over. Hung-over and wrung out. Hung-over, wrung out and tossed about. She glanced at her watch and saw that there were still three hours before they landed. That was three hours in which she might have been sleeping. Those sedatives must have a wake-up component. What a rip-off. Now, she felt cheated, and her vindictiveness returned to the men in her life, the men she most detested at this moment. Her father, her brother, and her husband. They all cheated her too, didn't they? Just like the medication, by not providing what she needed.

She tried to return to sleep, but it was too late. Or too early. Her body was completely confused. So were her thoughts. There was no logic. No rationale. Only retribution and rage. Only anger caged by the plane, delayed in time and experienced through the fog and filth of travel. She'd land, hire a taxi to take her to the hotel, freshen up, and call room service for a stiff drink. Then she'd find her brother.

CHAPTER 38
Setting the Stage

Mac decided it was better if his son, the unwelcomed intruder, discovered him working diligently on the boat, so he turned his attention to the mainsail winch that was loosening from the mast. Boats take work. There is always something to fix or fit. He brought the tools from the stow and began removing the lines, freeing the bolts, taking the winch plate apart, and strengthening the wood so that he could reverse the procedure and ensure the winch would work. Not only would his busywork look good for visiting eyes, he could hoist sail when he decided it was enough.

He worked for two hours, glancing sometimes at his watch, and wondering when his son would show. How long would it take to arrive from the airport? And if the flight were late, or if he'd gone to a hotel for a shower or a nap before launching into whatever diatribe he would start when he arrived, how long would that take? And if Michael knew the lying photographer told Mac of his son's arrival, would Michael delay just to cause agitation? You bet your ass he would, Mac thought. But the little shit doesn't win because I am fixing my winch.

After three hours passed, Mac was angry. He didn't have the time to sit around all day waiting for an unwanted, uninvited, ungrateful asshole to decide he was ready for a confrontation. There were things he wanted to do. Why should he wait? He didn't have an appointment. It was a surprise attack. Well, the surprise would be for his son when he showed up to the boat, and no one was there.

He finished bolting the winch, and as the epoxy needed time to harden, he went below, scrubbed his hands, grabbed his shirt, and headed toward the skiff. He went through this process thousands of times in the past years in Majorca. He checked to be sure the cabin electricity was off and that he had his wallet and his onshore bag. He climbed the steps, closed the cabin door, and scurried down the ladder to the dinghy. He left his boat often, and always with the same procedure, but on this day, he did something that wasn't a part of his Majorca ritual. He locked the cabin hatch.

———

CHAPTER 39
Sympathetic Counsel

When Mac hit the mainland, he headed directly to the café and arrived before the lunch crowd reached critical mass. Ernesto was relieved to see him.

"I am glad to see you're alive. When you left last evening, you looked upset."

"I was. I am. There is too much happening. On top of the discovery that the photographer I hired, who I thought would be a new friend, was actually a delegate sent from my family to track me down, and that an unwanted convergence is eminent, I proposed to Elizabeth last evening," Mac divulged to his Majorca friend. Ernesto was silent for a moment and then sat at the table with Mac. Given all the bar owner had to do, the action carried import. Mac watched Ernesto's assaying face.

"She is lovely," Ernesto said after sitting.

"Yes," Mac agreed. "But . . ." He sighed. "I don't know why I did it. The excitement, I suppose. From the day. The photos. From her saying 'Yes' to it all. A 'Yes' is food for a man, especially a hungry one. When a man has too much want, he throws caution to the wind. He begins to believe. In this instance, I believed myself. The hardest thing for a man to smell is his own crap."

"It is best not to put your nose in the commode," Ernesto agreed.

159

"Exactly," said Mac. "Yesterday, when I was at the boat getting ready, I looked through the photos we'd taken, and suddenly I thought of what it would be like when she left. When I was alone again. When I wasn't meeting, dancing, and planning with her. I know she agreed to impersonate my writer, and I knew we'd see each other, but I don't know, I just suddenly wondered if I cared for her. And if I did, what do I do? And then when I saw her, and we were walking over, and the world was uninterrupted, and there was the sky, and the night, and she was willing to believe . . . I just asked."

"You are a romantic, my friend. It is a beautiful thing to see. We can use more romance in this world. That is what my wife always says, though she does little to make it so. When you asked the beautiful Elizabeth, what did she say?"

"I took her by surprise. I could see it. She said she'd consider it overnight, but . . . I don't think she'll say yes. Especially after all the mess with this camera man."

"I am sorry I blurted it out," Ernesto atoned. "It was a moment of struggle, but I thought your knowing was better than not."

"Yes," Mac agreed. "It is blissful to be at sea and ignorant of approaching typhoons, but it is always best to have the life jackets at hand."

"Did you find him? Last night? The investigator?"

"He found me. After asking at hotels where he might likely have stayed, I headed back to the dock. He was sitting there, waiting. He confessed everything and told me my son was landing at eight this morning."

"Your son has come to Majorca?" Ernesto asked.

"That is what he told me."

"That is a great tribute," Ernesto recognized. "The investigator went to the dock to let you know, that shows respect."

"Or pity."

"It is difficult to not appreciate your character," Ernesto insisted, "even when I feel sorry for you." The men chuckled. "Don't think I often feel sorry for you," Ernesto added. "You have way too much excitement for sympathy." They laughed again, as men who know each other may, and then Ernesto steered the conversation toward the immediate news. "So, did you see your son? How did it go? How does he look after so many years? Was he glad to see you?" Ernesto asked.

"He hasn't presented himself," Mac reported with disdain. "He came all this way and hides; such is his love."

Mac had repeatedly said how glad he was to be unattached to his offspring, yet in the possibility's light, Ernesto sensed a certain melancholy in Mac. Failure creates longing. Ernesto understood. Wanting something, having it in reach, and then for it not to realize is the great tragedy of life. Even Ernesto knew this was true. Possible regret is a great killer of hope. No person remains untouched by that disappointment. It is often life's party favor.

"He will. Soon," Ernesto soothed. "Your son will find you soon. Do not worry." Ernesto only hoped the reunion was not painful. Family meetings can go either way, Ernesto thought. They can be treasures or tortures, and the outcome is usually unpredictable. He returned the subject to the other meeting, romance. That can be a treasure or a torture too. "And what of the beautiful senorita? What will you do?"

"I will go to her hotel," Mac decided. "I will tell her I was overwhelmed with her beauty last evening and spoke too much, too soon. That if she will consider a slight change of plan, say to continue for the next months as we had previously agreed, that we could investigate a stronger commitment then," Mac outlined.

"She will find that wise," Ernesto said.

"Unless she is madly in love with me and is heartbroken by the withdrawal."

"Women are never heartbroken by withdrawal," Ernesto said slyly. "It is often the preferred action."

Comforted by Ernesto's sensitive and sympathetic counsel, Mac finished his mid-day coffee and walked toward Elizabeth's hotel with at least the sense that he had a plan.

———

CHAPTER 40
Touching Ground

Beth always panicked when the plane began its final descent. There was something about the phrase "final descent" that sounded so fatalistic. From the moment the fasten seat belt light went on, and she could feel the plane coming down in altitude, fear took over. That concern kicked into high gear when the landing wheels lowered from the plane. She flinched when she heard them. All she could envision was a bird who has tucked its claws into its underside when in flight and then jettisons them forward when approaching their prey.

The last minutes were always white-knuckle ones for her, literally. She gripped the seat arms with such a fervor that the blood drained from her hands, and she pressed herself into the seatback cushion certain the plane would fall from the sky or skid out of control, and she'd end in a blazing fury with the clanging of emergency trucks and strangers escorting her soul into the ether. The worst was always the treacherous moment when the wheels touched the tarmac of the runway and bounced as one reality reached out to connect with another. It was as if two nannies fought for a child, and the child could only clutch to the air and wait for the fray to end. The best the child could hope for was that it wasn't dropped on its skull, and one of the caregivers was victorious.

It was always a relief when the drama concluded, and the plane rolled to a stop after jockeying for the gate. With the boarding bridge latched to the craft like a leech, that ridiculous bell chimed, and the jet purged itself of the passengers, both those with good and bad intentions.

Beth liked her feet solidly on the ground, even if her head was reeling. She put out a steadying hand as she strode down the gate ramp, glad to have the earth firmly beneath her feet once again. Well, as firmly as it could be given the circumstances. She wheeled her carry-on through the terminal, emerging into the Majorca sunshine and the tropical paradise, artificial or natural, that surrounded her, without so much as a single thought of the beauty.

The cab ride to the hotel held picture-perfect panoramas through each window, and the guide, a lovely and spirited driver, tried his best to point out sights and offer fascinating historical information in a clipped Spanish accent. "Welcome to Majorca. This is an island of magic. It was occupied by the Romans in 123 BCE under Quintus Caecilius Metellus Balearicus, a famous statesman. The island flourished, and Palma was established. Over two thousand years ago. Are you planning to see the beautiful center? Be sure to include the cathedral, and there is the castle. Real Castillo de Santa Catalina de Alejandria, also called St. Catherine's Castle. There is no charge to visit. It was built in 1554, to protect the city. And La Zarza. Ah, you must go. Traces of the ancient civilization of Benahoares were found there. So much to see. So much to do. Food, wine, song, And the beaches. Palma has beautiful beaches."

"Please be quiet," Beth said, "and drive."

Another snooty American, the driver thought. Always running off to be somewhere and never happy where they are. Americans are shit. The driver became quiet, and the joy he had in sharing his homeland with visitors was quelled. Ah, well, let her be as miserable as she wants to be, he decided. Whatever she gets is what she most likely deserves. They rode the rest of the way in silence.

They arrived at the hotel where she had hastily booked a room. The driver took her case from the trunk and handed it to the porter. "Watch out for this one," the driver whispered, then charged Beth twice the rate. When she refused to pay and began to haggle, the driver said, "No hablo English." She fumed but paid him, threatening to file a complaint.

The hotel porter, taking her bag, smiled his most winning smile and said, "Welcome to Palma."

"You live on a rock," Beth replied. "Why are you all so fucking happy?"

"Majorca is magic," the porter grinned.

"Yeah, and Disneyland is the happiest place on Earth," Beth chided and then strode into the hotel. The porter rolled his eyes and then wheeled the case after. Maybe, depending on how things went, just maybe, she'd look around and find out what made this place so intriguing to the locals. On the other hand, she may discover it was as it appeared, a massive rock of seasonally expensive nothing.

CHAPTER 41
The Ghost in The Placa Major

As Mac crossed the Placa Major on his way to Elizabeth's hotel, he wished he had a cell phone. He should call to let her know he was on his way. That would be the polite thing to do. It would also give her time to prepare. She could dress or practice her acceptance or refusal, whichever the result would be. But it didn't matter; he didn't have a mobile phone. He threw his into the Thames when his second wife left him.

Some people thought that his second wife's leaving was payback for his abandonment of his first. He didn't see it that way. He attributed the action to his second wife's bitchiness. When she left that day, he was angry and a little afraid. He knew his travels would never be the same. He loved twice and twice he was hurt. The berth and the boat were lonelier after being shared. He would not have it again. He would not allow it again. He would learn, and he would find solace in solitude. He pitched his phone into the murky waters under the London Bridge. Damn her, he thought, enticing, coaxing, and promising a tantalizing future of passion, only to discover her true ambition was to be a house frau. At the end of the month, he had hoisted anchor and left England for new adventure.

Throwing his cell phone away represented a complete separation from his previous life. Mac was always concerned that he could be tracked by satellite via his phone, so he changed it often, but for convenience he kept one. After his exit from London, he called only on pay phones or from phone-call stores in the cities where he docked. It confused most of his friends, but he didn't have that many, so what difference did it make?

The Placa Major has a long history, most notable for the Spanish Inquisition in Majorca until 1823. It is easy to visualize those violent tribunals when you enter the plaza. The surrounding buildings with ground-level arches likely made a great backdrop for destroying heretics. Now, it is a market of tourist-aimed trinket-vendors and pricey cafés, but still in the shadows of the recesses, in the darkened vaults, if you look closely, you can see the ghosts of those who suffered there. Martyrs and mercenaries, men and mistresses, heretics and dissenters; all suspected were tried, and those found guilty left their souls in that place. Even centuries later, their spirits are present, mixing with the bauble-hunters.

Crossing through the square was always a challenge during tourist season. A person needed a steady gait to avoid being trampled by vacationers desperate to experience the entirety of their trip through the screens of their idiotic smartphones. It was also vital to keep your eyes open. Placa visitors were mesmerized, searching through the "authentic" relics of the Inquisition that filled dozens of carts in the courtyard. Mac usually walked the long way around the throng, but he wanted to settle the question with Elizabeth, so he took the shortest route, directly through the square.

Suddenly, Mac's eye was drawn by a movement in one of the arches, and his heart raced. What was there? Standing in the arches? Who was that? Mac peered into the shadows, and he saw . . . a ghost. Mac was startled. He squinted and looked again. This was not some tourist catching the sun. This was an apparition. There was a white outline surrounding the shape of a person. Mac might have thought it was a trick of the light, a reflection from a window, or an odd beam that made its way through a passage he could not see, but the figure did not seem to stand on the ground. The figure seemed to hoover and shift, and the spirit was looking. Looking, as if searching through the crowd. Mac blinked, certain that when he looked again, the vision would be gone, but it wasn't. There was the phantom, still. Under the arches. Looking. Searching. Scanning the crows as if trying to find a specific soul among the throng. And then the spirit saw Mac, and Mac knew the demon was staring at him. There were hundreds of tourists milling about, but Mac could tell the vision was staring at him. Mac couldn't hide. There was no place to go. He knew there was no way to be unseen. Mac stepped forward and peered with intent back at the shadow. Then, he saw. It wasn't a ghost; it was his son. The figure in the arch was his son. Michael was probably on his way to the docks. On his way to surprise his father. How fortuitous, Mac thought, a level playing field. The game could end now. Then the figure shifted. Mac gasped deeply and shouted, "Hey." He ran, compelled by anger and fear, toward his son, shouting profanities as he went. "You shit. You little bastard. You punk." When he got to the darkened arch, he reached out to grab the apparition, but the specter vanished. Mac stood in the recess, sputtering, looking for a doorway into which his son could dart, a secret hiding spot, or even ectoplasm. His hands flew across the rock that made the building, feeling for some opening. Mac turned in every direction, scouring the area for some sign, some souvenir of the demon he just saw. Nearby tourists stopped as if witnessing a fit. Placa visitors stared, some with outrage, some with astonishment and some with compassion. Mac didn't mind the anger from the passersby, and he didn't mind the surprise. He was used to those; the compassion, however, hurt. Mac waved his hand as if to say, it is all right, and then he leaned against the building, breathing hard, and put his hand over his eyes.

When his heart stilled, Mac walked the rest of the way to the hotel, but he was unsettled by the experience. He kept checking behind him and scanning dark doorways along the path. Two tourists jolted out of a nearby store, and Mac jumped. They were apologetic, but he was angry. Not at the tourists. At his son. Even before his son made the first move, Michael put his father off balance. He would have a drink, Mac promised himself, after he visited Elizabeth. Elizabeth; the idea of his authoress inhabited brought him peace and hope. It amazed him how the thought of this woman made all hardships bearable. He could handle his son. Knowing Ms. Kensington was close made it seem simpler. Mac was eager to right the course of their friendship. And who knew? Who knew what that partnership might become? Consideration grows in time. And all passion starts with consideration.

He arrived at the hotel and took the elevator to Elizabeth's room. He stood outside the door, took off his hat, checked his shirt and smoothed his hair. Then he knocked. There was no response. He listened at the door but only heard silence. He knocked again and then quietly called out her name. "Elizabeth? Elizabeth?" He knocked once more. "Elizabeth?" There was nothing. He went downstairs to see if his fellow adventurer was in the dining room, but she was not. Then he went to the front desk.

"I'd like to leave a message for Ms. Schoenhauer," Mac said. The clerk looked up.

"Ms. Schoenhauer has checked out," the clerk reported.

"No, she is staying here for two more days," Mac said.

"She left this morning," the clerk informed, "some emergency, I believe. She had a visitor, an American, and after, she left."

"What American?" Mac asked in confusion.

"I am not certain. He called from the house phone and then went up. A few minutes later he left. And then Ms. Schoenhauer called to say she would be checking out."

"That is not possible." Mac was bewildered. "There must be some mistake," he said. "We had a date for this morning." He started to tell the clerk that he proposed to Elizabeth the night before, and he wanted to ask her if he could take back the suggestion. He would ask her again later, if they got along. Mac wanted to tell the clerk that he made a simple mistake. An error of passionate haste, and that he came that morning to make amends. Mac knew his explanation sounded chaotic, jumbled and misdirected, so he restrained himself and stood there, deflating like a punctured raft.

The clerk must have made his own conclusions, because he asked, "Are you Mac?"

"Yes," Mac said.

"She left this for you." The clerk reached behind the counter and handed Mac an envelope.

In the envelope was a note. It was simple and direct: "My dear Majorca Mac, I am sorry. Elizabeth."

———

CHAPTER 42
The Hand of the Son

Mac sat in one of the faded striped chairs in an out-of-the-way corner of the lobby, reading and re-reading the note. "I am sorry." Sorry. What did she mean? Sorry for throwing him aside? Sorry for running away? Sorry for derailing his plan, for kicking him in the stomach, for sending him into a spiral, into a vortex — again — again — again — a maelstrom pulling you under, suffocating you, drowning you. How many times can you swim to the surface and gasp for breath only to be pulled back under water? To look up and see the light but be too paralyzed to move? How often can you be blindsided before you scream? He did, he wanted to, to scream. Never trust a woman.

His mother was the first to betray him. She was psychotic, he determined. Three or four people in one. Casting him aside for the latest man. Leaving him in his room to hear the grunts and groans. Smoking later, after the "gentleman" left, telling her son she loved only him. And he believed her, he did, until the next man visited. And the next. And the next. Grunts and groans and always after, cigarettes.

The next was his first wife, doling out sex and draining his energy with her ambition for social appearance. And not supporting him in that difficult time after his boozed mistake. Fuck her, he thought. Oh, he and his wife made up in time. She said because she loved him, but likely it was because she didn't want to be left with nothing. And then, when they did separate, how she pitted the family against him. She always did that. "Poor me. Poor you. Horrible him." With her, it was always a wrestling match for sides.

And his second wife. Bitch, waiting till they were ready to leave London, then announcing that she was staying. Her family, her mother, her homeland. She found a man that she believed would take steadfast care of her. She stayed.

And now Elizabeth. Another walkout, another betrayal, another bitch. He didn't understand. He was confused. He agreed the proposal was untimely, but he was going to make that right. Why did she run away? Did he frighten her? Maybe he could find her and soothe the situation. He thought back through the short time they'd spent together. Was he too insistent, too exuberant, too romantic? He swam through the water of self-recrimination and then burst to the surface and gasped. "An American," the clerk had said.

CHAPTER 43
Rage and Ramble

Mac walked from the hotel in hopeless rage. An American? It must have been his son. Who else would meddle in his life? Who else would try to stop his happiness? Who else had flown half-way around the world to bring misery? If he could have reached his son, he would have tried to strangle him. Even now he looked for someone to vent his fury at. His usual "Isn't-it-a-beautiful-morning" beam became an aggressive, angry scowl. Passersby took a wide berth. Tourists avoided his stormy gaze. No one asked for directions.

Mac was perplexed as to what to do. He could run through the city once again, banging on hotel doors, looking for the interfering bastard. He could question clerks and porters for information that would point him to the place where his son was lodged. He could work himself into a frenzy and still come up empty-handed. Instead, he chose a more practical approach and stopped at a local bar en route for a shot of strategy. With the clarity that comes from tequila, he decided on peace and patience over panic and headed back to the bay and his boat, stopping at several other oases along the way to review his plan. His son would come to find him. He would come, if only to gloat. He would go back and wait. And when that little dumbass showed himself, Mac would be ready.

By the time he got to the dinghy, Mac was shifting sails between vindictive cursing and old sailing songs. He untied the skiff and chugged home. It was not until he pulled aside his ship that he saw Enrico, the son of Ernesto's cousin, who worked for a harbor boat rental. Enrico was sitting in a speedboat tethered to the ladder of Mac's boat. When Mac approached, the young man nodded toward the deck. Mac winked, tied up the dinghy, and climbed the ladder.

———————

CHAPTER 44
Unsatisfying Reunion

"What the hell do you think you are doing here?" Mac demanded when he climbed on board.

"Nice to see you too, Father." Michael was sitting on the deck box shaded from the sun by the bridge. Michael looked older since he and his father last saw each other. He had also gained weight. Not sloppy, but enough to notice. It had been twenty-five years. No one stays the same through that much time.

"Michael, I could have you arrested for boarding my boat without permission," Mac said.

"Do you want me to call the harbor patrol for you?" Michael offered.

"It's a violation of maritime law, you know," Mac persisted. "You could be arrested for piracy."

"That would require there was something here of value to plunder, wouldn't it?"

"You have no right to just come on board when you want."

"I would have waited on the doorstep, but oh right, you don't have one," Michael returned. The pissing was a hint of the stifled anger neither man was yet ready to let explode. They were silent for a moment as they sized each other up.

"You got fat," Mac said, moving to the mast.

"I eat too much," Michael said. "You look thin."

175

"The boat takes a lot of work." Mac pretended to check the winch and the repairs he worked on earlier.

Michael looked around. "It needs a lot of mending."

"I just said that, didn't I? I said it was a lot of work."

"You said it takes a lot of work. I am saying it needs a lot of work."

"I work on it all the time," Mac said in defense. "Just today, I worked on the winch."

"And you didn't finish the job," Michael noted.

"It takes time for the epoxy to dry, Michael," Mac said.

"If you kept up with it before it splintered, it wouldn't need the time," Michael prodded.

"Not here two minutes and already you are criticizing. 'You didn't do this. You didn't do that.' You get that from your mother, you know." Mac was irritated. "Never good enough. Always something wrong." Even after all this time, his father could say just the right thing to make Michael boil. The invading son started to speak but took a deep breath instead, and the two men sat in petulant silence. The sound of the waves in the bay filled the space between them. Mac leaned against the mast.

"Have you been drinking?" Michael asked.

"I'm seeing my son for the first time in twenty-something years," Mac defended. "Unannounced, I might add. Unannounced, uninvited and unwanted. A shot of courage in anticipation of this great reunion is understandable."

It was understandable, Michael thought. He only wondered if his father's intoxication was solely the result of the unique situation. He remembered how much his father enjoyed a strong drink, and

Michael wondered if drunkenness was a daily practice. "Is it a custom in this country to drink throughout the day?" Michael asked.

"Don't be a prig," Mac said. "Americans are such hypocrites. You have drunken lunches, alcohol before dinner, and nightcaps for sleep. There is one difference. In the United States, you drink because you hate life. Here, you drink because you love life."

"Is that it, Father? You were drunk in America because you hated your life, and now you are drunk because you love your life?"

"That shows the wondrous effect of drinking," Mac said. "It transforms you. You ought to try it. You might be happier."

"I am happy. I am perfectly happy. I didn't come here to talk about my happiness," Michael said.

"Well, why did you come?" Mac asked in defiance. "Why did you hire an investigator and have me tracked down, halfway around the world no less, and then send him to worm his way into my life? Oh, yes, I found out about him. Did you think I wouldn't figure it out? What did you tell him about me?"

"I didn't tell him anything," Michael said evenly. "Only that you were my father and disappeared, and that I wanted to find you."

"Why?" Mac demanded. "What were you hoping to find? You have no right to just hunt me down. To come here and put yourself in the middle of my life again. You have interfered with everything. All the plans. All the happiness. Everything was moving in the right direction, and you have made a mess." Then Mac roared, "What did you say to Elizabeth?"

So, he came to it, Michael thought. It was the girl. With his father, he supposed, it was always the girl. Always a woman. "She told me you proposed to her," Michael reported.

"So? What if I did?" Mac pressed.

"You only met her."

"Did your spy report hourly?"

"Often enough to piece the story together," Michael said.

"We were having great fun, Elizabeth and I," Mac said.

"I am sure. Fun and games until the truth comes out," Michael chided.

"What truth?" Mac protested. "I swear if you told her a bunch of lies . . ."

"I didn't need any lies, Father," Michael insisted. "You supplied plenty of them. A book? A writer? A con game? Pulling her into your scheme? Do you think she would never catch on? What did you expect would happen when you got tired of this one? When you didn't follow through? When she realized you would never really care for her? Or when no one wanted your book?"

"I'm a good writer," Mac said.

"A book? What do you know about writing?" his son replied. "You haven't even written a postcard since you abandoned your family. You're a cog salesman."

"What did you say to her?" Mac demanded again.

"I told her you were a shit," Michael yelled. "I told her you were a reckless husband and a bad father. I told her you were self-centered and did not know how to love anyone. That is what I remember from those years before you left. I told her how you loved the idea, the illusion of romance, the fascination of flirtation, but that when the chips are down, when it truly comes to taking a stand, you are undependable and will change course with the wind. I told her she could save herself the heartbreak because when it came right down to it, you could never love anyone but yourself."

"So that is why she left Majorca. You did it."

"That would be great, wouldn't it, Father, if I was to blame, but I wasn't. After I finished the abbreviated list of your unredeemable qualities, she thanked me and told me that nothing I said made any difference to her. She already arrived at the same conclusion and decided to leave."

Mac was slashed. "You're lying."

"Is it hard to believe that someone you only met could see through you? Father, when you take off the colored glasses, it is easy to see you have no idea what love is."

"I know what love is," Mac said.

"How?" Michael asked. "Have you changed, Father? Have you somehow been transformed? You don't love people; you love the dream. You fight armies of enemies, real or imagined, and overcome all obstacles pursuing the dream. You meet a woman, like Mother, and that woman becomes your hope, and you fall in love with the hope, and you think it is the woman. Isn't that what you did with Mother? And then when you are weary of the fight, or when the obstacles are more stubborn than you are ready for, you abandon the dream and choose another. Perfect life — gone. Perfect family — gone. Perfect business — gone. And it starts all over. But you forget there are others who get hurt. Others who believe in you and buy into your plans regardless of how unrealistic they are. You sell hope to people. And they buy. And they hope. And they tie their hope to yours until you walk out on them. The plan, the hope, and the people. What about the people? What about them? My mother? Your second wife? Your children? Your mother? You sap the love from the people around you so that you can believe in yourself."

Mac inhaled with pain. He felt the sting. "That is rich coming from a pampered mama's boy. What do you know about love?"

"I am still with my wife and children," Michael said. "I have not run out on them."

"Oh, so this is it," Mac said. "A chance to tell me one more time of all the things I did. To tell me how I disappointed you and your brother and your sister. How I bullied you. How I oppressed your mother. How rotten I was as a father." There was another pause as the waves of the emotions of a lifetime of sorrow ebbed. "That's why you came all this way," Mac concluded, "isn't it? One more chance to feel sorry for yourself."

"I don't feel sorry for myself," Michael objected.

"You had everything," Mac said. "There was nothing you were not given. You, or your brother, or your sister. The best. Always the best. Ever since you were born. And even when I left, you were not left without. There was plenty for any need, so you had better not feel sorry for yourself. You have no right to feel sorry for yourself."

Michael waited while his father's vindictive reasoning dissipated on the harbor breeze, then he asked, "Why did you divorce Mother?"

"Oh. She's always at the center of it, isn't she?" Mac pointed out.

"She is my mother," Michael reminded.

"Yes, she is. And who could ever forget it? The moment you might, she was there to remind you. She would always remind you that she conceived you, she carried you, and she gave birth to you. She would point out that she took care of you, and she would always be there for you. Because she was your mother.

"But you didn't know her. Not the real her. You only saw the side of her she wanted you to see. The poor over-worked, under-loved, beleaguered and will-trudge-on-in-spite-of-the-hopelessness victim that she wanted you to think she was," Mac said. "It was how she kept everyone on her side. Playing that part. The woeful, worried, worn, worst, unhappy, giving-all-she-had-for-you woman. But it wasn't her. That was not the woman who pretended to be the steadfast but delicate matriarch. Your mother was not fragile. She was iron.

"Women are wonderful at weaving the story they want you to believe," Mac continued. "Don't forget, I had my own mother. Your grandmother was a master of manipulation. She could turn any moment to her dramatic advantage. Her vices, her villainies, her vanity . . . she had them all for me, and all because of me. That is how a woman keeps the reins. That is how she entraps. Her every breath is for you, because of you. It isn't her. It is all you. For love. All because she loves you. Does that sound familiar?"

A flash of recognition went through Michael's mind. He could see the similarity in the description. Some years after his mother died, he began to wonder what was in the shadow behind the light. Time creates distance; sometimes, it takes distance to see. Looking at the past from now, he thought of his mother, certain actions she took, odd phrases he remembered, and they made him wonder if his mother felt the maternal beatitude that he thought she did. She was kind to Michael. She lavished him with love and attention. Maybe she was not kind to Father. Michael could see how it was better to be the receiver of her care than her disregard.

"Your grandmother held on as tightly as she could," his father went on. "And when I met your mother, I thought I would be free; that I was moving on to a warm and loving partnership. It wasn't just because your mother was beautiful, but because she had such refined edges. Grandma was coarse and callous and as cutting as a razor. Your mother was pretty, well-spoken, well-mannered and charming. And I was beguiled. I was blinded. At first. For several years. It was only later, after . . . after the family began to grow, that I saw, with horrifying shock, the two women were almost exactly the same. And even with all of that, even with the twist of a silent scream in my throat, even with the knowing that I married the sort of woman I did not want, even then I loved her."

"So, why divorce her?" Michael asked.

Mac looked over the worn deck, to the beaten rails, and out to the sea, and he suddenly felt tired. "She stopped loving me." He sat on the cabin window hull. "Maybe she never loved me. I thought she did. I truly believed she did. And I think I loved her. But at some point, I realized I was only enchained, that her love came with so many capitulations and constraints, that it was only more negotiation, then I just wanted to be free. She captured my heart and was strangling my soul. That is not a promising life. I wanted to feel excited about the future again." There was a pause in the conversation as each considered what was said and what was heard.

"You didn't come to the funeral," Michael stated.

"That was your sister. She made it clear that I was not wanted," Mac said.

"She never said that," Michael insisted.

"If she told you she never said that, she is lying to you."

"I don't think she'd lie about something like that," Michael said.

"Yes, she would. And she wouldn't think twice. She's had a lot of practice lying. It makes her immune to guilt," Mac said. "A lie is more than just a manipulation; it's a shift in morality. After so many lies, after so much shifting, you can't distinguish the truth. Worse, you don't even mind that you can't tell the difference anymore. For you, the lies are the truth and damn anyone who challenges them."

"And then marrying that beach girl," Michael said with disdain.

"That turned out to be a problem, didn't it?" Mac said. "But how was I to know that at the beginning? Any relationship is a roll of the dice. It might have been lifelong love."

"She was thirty years younger than you. How did you think that would work out?" Michael asked wryly.

"The idea was rejuvenating," Mac said.

"It was juvenile," Michael stated. "Midlife crisis part two. And to take it out on Mother?"

"You don't know what it's like," Mac said, "to work every single second of your life for someone else. Never a thing for yourself, always for your children, always for your mother, always for your wife. When I left, when I finished this ship and packed the clothes, I said from that moment on, I would live for myself. But your mother had other ideas. She was happy to sail as long as the course was hers. And if you want something else, you hold it in. You hold it in, and you think you can make it through one more day. And then one more day goes by, and you believe you can do it for one more, and then one more, and then one more until you feel that if you don't do something, you will just die. I did something. I left your mother, I divorced her and married badly. And then it was the same all over again. Doing it again, for someone else, always for someone else. Why is it always for someone else? Sure, they try to make you feel it isn't that way, but it is. The choices you make, the course you set, every breath you take, you do it for them. Always for them. Why can't it be for me?"

"Isn't that love?" Michael asked in agitation.

"I don't know," Mac said. "But I wanted more."

"You always wanted more. Always. It was never enough for you, was it?" Michael said.

"No!" Mac shouted. "No! Can't a man have more? Why does a person have to settle for affection given out in measured portions like food at a soup kitchen? Begging for more, wanting more, needing more. I worked. I worked hard. I provided for her, for you, for your brother and your sister. And every one of you resented my wanting something for myself. Why does that make me bad?"

Michael stood. "I don't know why I came," he said. "I just thought — I just wanted to see — I wanted to . . . He sighed heavily and started toward the ship's ladder, then he stopped and turned. "One thing more," Michael said, "and then I won't bother you again. Just one thing. I wasn't going to ask. I wasn't going to bring it up, but this may be the only time we talk." Michael stopped to summon his nerve and then asked, "When you molested Beth, did you know it was her?"

Mac thought the conversation would turn in this direction. He was sure the subject would arise, ever since he heard that his family was trying to find him. His son wanted to gnaw once more on that opaque night all those years ago when, in a drunken haze, and in the darkness of an unlit room, he reached out and touched his daughter. To have all the screams and the accusations once more reverberate in his mind. The echoes. The ghosts. Why did his son come? Why did Michael haunt him? To search through decades and distance, for what? For some assurance that the family indeed indicted him correctly?

"If I tell you I did not, will you believe me?" Mac asked.

Michael thought for a moment and then went down the ladder to the dinghy to take him to shore.

———

―――――――

CHAPTER 45
Beth at the Hotel

Beth was relieved to reach her hotel room. She thought that if she ran into one more smiling housekeeper or bowing bellhop who told her how welcome she was in Majorca, she couldn't be responsible for her actions. When did service workers come to believe they were a part of the conversation? Who cared what they thought? Who cared if the waitress was pleased you were eating at that restaurant? What happened to customer service where the service workers actually left you alone? She hated it when she went to dinner, and the server interrupted a dozen times to make sure everything was perfect. She often wanted to snap back, "The food is ordinary, the lighting is unflattering, but the most annoying thing in this experience is you. Please go away."

Alone at last, she pulled the drapes on the window to minimize the cheery sunlight and snatched a bottle from the minibar. How dreary, she thought, a minibar; was there anything as classless as a pay-by-the-piece minibar? Whatever magic the locals thought Majorca had, it was just a tourist trap with old buildings. A rack of postcards in the hotel lobby that featured beautiful beaches and panoramic mountain views were likely old enhanced photographs. Hotels were notorious for posting appealing and sparsely inhabited poolside pictures, only for a visitor to find swarms of children and alcohol-sodden young adults crammed into every square inch. Still, she might look around before she returned home. First, she'd take care of business. She'd finish her drink and go into the bathroom to rinse off the travel debris. Then she'd put on fresh clothes and find the hotel where her brother, the bastard, was staying.

* * * * * * *

Michael returned to shore with a stony face that did not match the turbulence he felt in his heart. Why did he come? What did he expect would happen? Did he think his father would fall to his knees in tears and beg to be forgiven? How easy that would have been. Michael would have been free to dole out judgment or mercy as he felt, and the whole chapter would have been completed. Closed. Finished. He should have known his father would not capitulate easily. No contrite reform. No pleading for mercy from the court. No answers. Only questions. More questions. Anger and hate, even misplaced, are a respite to uncertainty.

What surprised Michael most was how acrimonious his father was. There was no remorse, no regret, only a faraway echo of fury about all that he felt he missed. Michael could feel his father's quiet rage, a rage born of all that had been strangled from him, all the hope that had been suffocated when he married and became a parent. What dreams had his father given up? What dreams had Michael given up himself? Life is always choice. With each choice comes a surrender of some dream. You'll never backpack across Europe. You'll never run with the bulls or leap off a cliff into the ocean spray. You don't give up the guitar, but it sits gathering dust until one day, years later, you put it into a box with your ambitions and drop it at a local thrift store. You are not instantly filled with regret.

That comes later when you see a concert, or a sidewalk performer, and you wonder if the dream they seek is worth the living they eke. And how would you have done anyway? Would you have been the next great light or another star that did not blaze?

When he got to the shore, he paid for the dinghy and headed for his hotel, but he did not leave his feelings dockside. With each step, he thought of his father and all the things said on the boat. Had his mother been as harsh as his father described? No child can know the woman who bore him in the same way her husband may. People are apt to change to fit the balance of a relationship, but how could two views be so varied? A loving and selfless mother to him, a manipulative and cold-hearted wife to his father. It was as if one person, a single photograph, was fractured, the view shifting with the onlooker.

Michael never realized how unhappy his father was. And not just because of his relationship with his mother, but his grandmother as well. How could the warm, loving grandmother that he remembered, the one who baked cakes and gave kisses and chocolate-covered graham crackers, be the same cold, harsh woman his father described? How little did Michael know his grandmother? How little did he know his mother? How little did he know himself?

His father looked old. His blustering outrage could not hide an undercurrent of frailty. And the boat was in disrepair. That was so unlike the father he remembered. The father he remembered could not rest until every last detail was complete. He was always fixing and tweaking and reworking and rearranging so that even the simplest thing was exactly as he thought it should be. It was true, his father was driven by hubris, but he was driven. This man careening on the deck after drinking his way across the city of

Palma, this man who spoke through a haze, and whose eyes glazed with armor in preparation of a face-to-face with eldest forgotten son, this man, this estranged, eccentric, seafaring father, was not the man he was expecting to find when he came to Majorca.

When Michael made it back to his hotel, he was filled with more doubt than ever before. What if he had spent all these years seeing his father through the viewfinder of propaganda perpetuated by his mother? He remembered standing in the hallway next to Mother that night when the light illuminated his father with his sister. He saw his father's hands cupped hungrily around his sister's breasts. He remembered the surprise and the confusion on his father's face. He took that for guilt. His mother reinforced the judgment by saying things like, "Your father is not a bad man," or "When he drinks, he does things." She never said it directly, but it was clear that his mother thought her husband was guilty. Michael remembered Beth's face, startled and scared, but somehow defiant and challenging. It was a hint of the aggressive and unhappy woman she would become. A woman who always has to be at the center of attention, and who, in time, would make everyone around her pay homage. Expectant and petulant, and somehow as if she had gotten things to work out exactly as she wanted, that was the face he remembered. Suddenly that face was standing before him, in the lobby of his hotel in the far-away magical island of Majorca.

"Beth?" Michael asked with surprise.

"I haven't died since we spoke yesterday, if that's what you mean," she retorted.

"No, I'm just . . . well, shocked. What are you doing here?" Michael inquired.

"Did you think I was going to let you get away with it?" Beth accused.

"Get away with what?"

"Don't even try it," said Beth. "I know about the whole plan. I know exactly what you are up to."

The desk clerk had been eyeing Beth with concern ever since she made her stormy entrance into the lobby to wait for her brother. Now, he stepped forward. "Excuse me," he said. "Is everything all right?"

"It is not all right," said Beth, "and I'll kindly ask you to keep out of it. This is a family matter."

"And this is the lobby of a hotel. Perhaps a more discreet location would be appropriate for your discussion," the concierge suggested.

"Of course," said Michael. "Come up to my room," he said to Beth. "We'll have a drink and sort this out, all right?"

"Fine," said Beth, "but I don't understand how everyone on this God-forsaken rock can be so idiotic." Michael took her by the arm, and they made their way to his room. The muzzle lasted only until the door closed.

"Your place is nicer than mine," Beth squawked. "At least you've got a bar with booze. My room has a minibar." She walked directly to the liquor and poured herself a scotch. "You want one?" she said to Michael.

"I'm not sure yet," Michael responded. "What is going on?"

"It took me a while to figure it out," said Beth. "I am so stupid. You fly across the world to hunt down a father who abandoned us years ago. And, on the phone, when I ask you why you were going, you say something inane about just wanting to see him. Nice try. Frankly, I am more hurt than angry by what you are trying to do."

"What is it you think I am trying to do?" Michael asked.

"Take the money."

"What money?"

"The money Dad has stashed," Beth spewed.

"You think I tracked him down and flew all the way here because Father has a secret stash somewhere?"

"Of course. Money is the only thing that ever mattered to you. It's the only reason you would go through all this. Where is it? Have you talked with him yet? It must be a large amount. I want half. At least. I was the one he molested," Beth summarized.

Michael stared. He was speechless. He didn't know whether he should laugh or weep. Either way, he could certainly understand why his father was not eager to engage with his children. He wanted to tell his sister that she was awful. He wanted to tell her that she was hard and unfeeling. He wanted to tell her that she was stupid and horrible. He didn't. He just looked at her sadly. "Father doesn't have any money, Beth."

"You'll say anything, won't you," she started, "just to keep it all for yourself."

"Beth, listen to me. There is no stockpile of bonds and cash. There is no hidden fortune. Father has his pension, but it is a small amount, and that is all there is."

"You're lying," she jabbed at Michael. "You're lying."

"He is old. He is frail. It looks as if he lives hand to mouth. He gets by somehow, and he still enjoys drinking, but there is no stash. The boat is falling to ruin. He is alone. He has no one. There was a girl. That part of him hasn't changed. This woman he'd met only three days ago, and he proposed, but she has left."

"How do you know all this?"

"The private detective. I am partly to blame. The woman is at least thirty years younger than Father. I went to see her this morning. To talk to her, to tell her about Father," Michael said.

"Did you tell her he was an insane narcissist who drove his wife to death and ran away from his family?" Beth scoffed. "Did you tell her to turn and run? Did you tell her that there have been enough fortune hunters in this family already, and we would not tolerate another?"

"I went to her hotel and told her what I felt about our father and his behavior. I gave her a complete history of his failure with relationships. I pointed out his constant shifting moods and his evaporating goals, but nothing I said mattered. She had already decided to forget Father and leave Majorca," Michael reported.

"And I'm glad of it," Beth snarled. "The last thing I need is to split my share with anyone."

"Beth, there is nothing," Michael repeated. "If you think I am lying, why don't you go and see for yourself?"

"You don't expect me to go and talk to him, do you? To beg him to do the right thing?"

"Go see the boat and decide for yourself. He is moored at the harbor. You can't miss the boat. Look for the one about to sink. If you are uncertain, ask anyone there. Tell them you are looking for Mac. They all know him as Mac. If you still believe I am lying, and Father is hiding a fortune, you can have it all. I don't want it," Michael said in despair. "I don't want anything." He sat forlornly on the bed as if the simple act was more than he could manage. He put his hands over his face.

Beth eyed Michael suspiciously. "All right," she said. "I will." She picked up her purse and walked out of the hotel.

———

———

CHAPTER 46
Tanked

Mac sat on the deck for a long time after Michael departed. He watched his son's skiff skim across the early evening surf. A review of your life is supposed to last for a second, but now image after image and sound bite after sound bite washed over Mac in what felt like an eternity. A world of joy and heartbreak flooded over him like a giant storm surge. His wife, his life, the births of his children, never knowing his father, the death of his mother, building the boat, sailing — in bits and pieces and in epic segments, he revisited all. And it was cruel. So much hope, so many expectations, such dark despair, too great a sadness. All at once, all in a moment, all in watching that boat sail to the shore and disappear into the boat crowded bay. So much loss, all again. Life is difficult enough the first time, he thought, reflection is too much agony for anyone to suffer.

Watching Michael's boat vanish, Mac saw his lifetime fade into the massiveness of the universe. A dot. Swallowed in the cosmos. At this moment, Mac's past seemed insignificant and infinitesimal and innately useless. It was all a piss in the ocean. How sad. All of the fight, all of the tears and struggle, only a piss.

He finally stood up, unlocked the hatch, and went downstairs to make coffee. He went through his usual routine, filling the pot with water from the hold, adding the grounds, and putting the percolator on the stove. He released the valve to the propane tank and lit the burner. The temperamental tank refused to yield, so Mac gave it a customary whack. Suddenly, flames shot up and spread across the stove top. He reached for a towel and tried to beat them out, but the towel ignited on fire, burning, flaming. Lap by lap, the yellow tongues leapt to taste unexplored territory. Each devoured the next frontier. One by one, the inferno grew as if the past was being incinerated by the present.

He threw the towel aside, trying to keep his mind on the task, but the towel fell against a wooden panel by the sink, and the cabinet below started to smoke then erupted in a flash. Every repair he had not accomplished, every task he had not completed, every dream he had not lived danced in the conflagration. He reached out to contain it, but the fire took hold of his shirt and started to burn. He screamed and cursed, batting his arm against the counter, trying to end the devouring blaze. With blistering pain, he grabbed for the fire extinguisher but lost his balance in the reach and fell. On the floor, the flames grew around him. Like Dante in the Inferno, he descended lower and lower till he was certain he would be consumed by the fire. Well, too bad, he thought. Too bad. He would never dance again, he would never spend another night with a woman, he would never see another sunrise. Oh well, too bad. No, he decided. Not like this. Death might come, but not like this. He summoned strength from the adrenaline of "never" and hoisted himself up the kitchen wall, manned the fire extinguisher, and subdued the demon.

When the fire was out, and he caught his breath, he surveyed the galley. There was damage. More damage. More to add to his list. More to take care of. More work to do. More, more, more. And then he felt the sting. On his hand, on his arm, and on his face. He realized he was scorched, and then he blacked out.

———

_____

CHAPTER 47
Great Expectations

Beth left the hotel and hailed a cab that was in line waiting for passengers. "The harbor," she told the driver.

"Si, senora," the driver responded. That was a mistake, she thought. The driver would not be receiving a generous tip from her. He should have called her senorita. She would have suspected it was bull, but she would have preferred to correct him herself. Why are all the people in this country so rude, she wondered as the taxi took off through the difficult flow of traffic that seemed to be a city-wide challenge.

As they moved through the labyrinth of narrow streets and the crush of close buildings, Beth was filled with contradictory thoughts. Was Michael telling the truth? Did she come all this way on some wild pretense? Or was Michael trying to stall her, buying himself time for some fast footwork?

She didn't want to see her father, not really. During years of therapy, she came to terms with what happened, and she'd given all the forgiveness she could find. There was none left for him now. He ruined her life once on that awkward and unforgettable night, then a second time by taking her mother away, and then a third time when Mother had died. If he hadn't built that boat. If he hadn't sailed away. If he hadn't cheated, Mother would still be alive. At least Father, out of guilt and shame, conceded to her demand and did not attend the funeral services. Beth didn't know what she would have done if he refused to cooperate. Threatened him, probably. Struck him, absolutely. Accused, remonstrated, admonished, cried . . . Oh, yes, she could make a scene when she wanted to. She had lots of theatricality to share with Father, but there would be no forgiveness. She had enough. Enough of wishing, enough of wanting, enough of worrying. He took everything from her. That was how she felt. And he owed her. A stack of cash couldn't make up for the past, but it was a start. She would think of additional retribution later. She didn't really wish him ill. Not exactly. All she wished him was an eternity of burning in Hell.

She was angry with her brother, as well. She did not want to exile him to an eternity of damnation, but a few years seemed perfectly reasonable to her. How ridiculous of him to go through this huge charade, to raise her hopes that there was a stash of money. And if there wasn't, which she did not believe, then why did he come all this way? What is the point? She tried to remember exactly what he said to her on the phone. "Unfinished business. I just want some — I don't know — satisfaction," he had said. "Closure."

Michael hired a private investigator to find her father. Just for satisfaction? How unlikely. He flew across the globe for closure? That was ridiculous. No wonder her suspicions were aroused. Maybe her brother said it all deliberately to hook her in, or maybe to shut her out. That was likely the intention. Michael jumped on the situation, and figured he'd get to the island, pump Dad's conscience, and then take the money and run. Michael sounded convincing when he claimed that there was no money, but . . . the shithead protested too much. Who believes anyone when they are so insistent? Well, she'd know soon enough. She'd arrive at the harbor, ask around and find the boat, and then she would decide for herself the best course of action. Maybe she'd wait for the right moment and make a public accusation of molestation. Or maybe she'd tell Father she missed him so and cry a bucket of tears. It really all depended on what she discovered at the harbor.

It took only a few minutes to get to the promenade. But Beth didn't have to worry about asking anyone where the boat was anchored. The dock was busy with activity as medics were looking after a man who had apparently suffered severe burns in a fire. In the distance she could see a cloud of smoke hanging over one of the boats. Moving through the crowd for a better look, she could see the boat with the loitering smoke. She was not certain, but it looked like her father's boat. Now alarmed and curious, she pushed her way into the frenzied activity surrounding the ambulance. The man being put on a stretcher had been in a fire. His arm and hand were scorched. The side of his face bubbled with red blisters. Some areas of his skin were black, and at certain spots, where the flesh was burned away, you could see the muscle and vessels. Even from the place she was standing, she could smell the charred skin, a mix of ammonia and charcoal. She wanted to move closer, but she needed no further confirmation. She knew instantly; it was her father.

Waves of confusion washed over her, and she thought she might vomit. Her father was unconscious but must be in searing pain. Oh, Good Lord, she thought, he had been burning in Hell. Her father had been in Hell. And she felt pity.

Pity is a strong emotion. Maybe because, at least for a moment, the horror you see jolts you out of yourself. In that instant, you are focused on someone other than yourself and are too numb to protect your feelings. And once you stop protecting yourself, once you let your guard down, the gate swings, and the way is open for all the secrets, the guilt, shame, jealousy, and hurt that have been sealed away. That must have been what happened, for Beth's mind flooded with emotions and memories that were locked in a carefully protected vault.

She was six years old, and she was looking at Father, thinking how handsome he was, and that when she was older, she wanted a boy that was just like him. And then she was eight, and she was watching him as he entertained a group of friends on the patio at their house. Father would say something clever, she supposed, and then everyone would laugh. And then she was ten, and she was going to a school dance and had put on her best and newest dress, and Mother had tied a ribbon in her hair, and her father had seen her and smiled with pride, telling her she was beautiful. And then he hugged her, and she felt cherished and important, and secretly — a secret she had never told anyone — secretly she loved him. Not like a daughter, but something else. Silly children, she thought. So young and gullible. So full of hopeless dreams. All little girls have those kinds of feelings for their fathers. They grow out of them. They don't mean anything. Not a thing. But even though that is what she wanted to believe, and even though she could deny it to everyone, she could not lie to herself. She was a little in love with him. And then she remembered that a long time before that night of light and accusation, she remembered that she saw her mother kiss her father, and she was furious and jealous.

She watched now as the gurney was placed into the ambulance. The siren sounded, and the medics headed off. Then she tried to catch her breath. But she could not. Her heart raced, and she thought she would faint. She picked up her cell phone and called her brother, wanting him to answer, needing him to answer, willing him to answer. To her anguish, he did not answer. She did not leave a voice message; she called the front desk of the hotel and asked to be put through to Michael's room, but he did not answer there either. She called the hotel again and asked for the desk. The concierge said he did not know where Mr. MacNeal had gone and asked if she would like to leave a message. "Yes," she gasped. "Tell him his father has been in a boating fire and has been taken to the hospital."

She disconnected before the clerk could respond and stood there, trying to stop her mind from spinning. Dazed and dizzy, she could not stand there for another moment, so she ran for the next taxi she saw. She would go to her hotel, she decided. She would gather her belongings, book the next flight back to America, and she would never again set foot on this island of Majorca.

CHAPTER 48
Michael at Dinner

Michael was so irritated by his sister that he could not sit in his hotel room. After Beth left to go to the dock, he went to a nearby cantina for a drink and a meal. In part, he was still disturbed by his visit with his father. In part, he was baffled by his sister's selfish appearance in Majorca. And in part, he didn't want to be at the hotel when his sister discovered the truth at the harbor. He was certain she'd return and take out her disappointment on him. That was how his sister was. She always blamed everything that happened to her on someone else.

Michael tried to talk to her, he tried to tell her the truth, but Beth never listened. She always insisted on being right, even when the facts proved otherwise. His father was like that too, Michael thought. He needed to be right about everything. Even when common sense showed that another plan of action was more sensible, his father refused to concede. That stubbornness had set the stage for altercations that exploded into stormy arguments. Those arguments were a big part of the polarization of the family. Taking sides, even in simple instances, was a declaration of alliance. It did not make sense to Michael. Why have conflict when there is a world between right and wrong? Collaboration, cooperation, and compromise were not often experienced in his family's house.

Sitting at the restaurant table, Michael sipped on a glass of wine and tried to still his thoughts. His mind would not cooperate. The turbulence stirred by the events of the day swirled.

He thought about his father and his sister and their insistence on always being right. His brother, Jonathan, had avoided that characteristic. Jonathan had ideas and opinions, but he never insisted that his views were the only ones, or the best ones. In the earlier adolescent years, Michael had seen his brother's passiveness as a weakness. But as time went on, Michael realized that there was strength and compassion in his brother's détente. There was no issue that had only one outcome, not one outcome so vital that you must fight with your family the way Beth and his father did, and . . . and his mother. All at once, Michael realized his mother had been like that too. She could not acquiesce with grace. She could never be wrong. And if things did not go the way she wanted, there was a storm. Sometimes it was choppy waters, sometimes it was a blustery gale, but there was always a repercussion if she did not get her way. He never thought of her in that way before. His mother, his sister, and his father; there was a lot of rightness in his family. Was he like that, he wondered? Did he need to be right? Maybe it was a genetic trait they all shared, some flaw in the family DNA.

As Michael sat in the dark restaurant, replaying the late afternoon patriarchal reunion. Him, his father, the boat, the discord. Michael came for satisfaction, some resolution. He wanted a purge. He wanted to shout and blame, to point and accuse. He wanted his father to know how badly he acted as a parent. For his father to say that he missed his son. Michael wanted to feel warmth, to think his father was pleased to see him. Ha, he thought.

Whatever Michael had bargained for, he came up short. He felt no satisfaction and no closure. He had come to Majorca, he supposed, to let go of all the suppressed feelings about his father, about his family, about his younger years. He wanted to package up all those feelings and all those memories, as a person might vacation photos or mementos of a romance, and then place them in a closed box with a large sign that said, "Do Not Open." He wanted to hide the box in the basement and let it collect dust. And then when he died, let someone else go into his things and throw the box out. Let them throw everything away without opening the lid, toss the box into a dumpster or burn it on a fire. Those seemed the best options for the past.

When he went to the harbor, he hoped, in his heart, that his father would say, "I'm sorry, son." And then Michael would say, "It's OK, Dad. I understand." But Michael didn't understand. His father wanted no release. His father felt he owed no explanation and no justification. His father wanted no forgiveness, no absolution. His father wanted nothing from his son. Nothing from his son. Did not want his son. His father did not want his son. That was a dissonance that pierced Michael, reminding him of all those years of pretending to be a part of a loving family.

It was clear to Michael that his father did not want his son, not now and not when Michael was younger. Michael felt his father did not want children, as if children were a burden, a responsibility that impeded life. That is hard on a child. Children do not understand. They appear and bring love. It is confusing when, instead, they find resentment or indifference, thought Michael. A child carries that with him for life, wanting to be loved, needing to be acknowledged, desperate to be accepted. And there is nothing to be done about it; you cannot force someone to care.

Michael often wondered what he did to make his father so uncaring toward him. Did he say the wrong thing? Make the wrong choice? Take the wrong action? What was the exact moment when his father decided not to love him? Was it when he was born? Was it when he was ill as a child? Was it the expense? The trouble? Did his father's disregard happen in one moment? Did his father awake one day and think, I do not want this child? Or did it occur little by little? Maybe it happened in a series of disappointments that took place through years. Maybe Michael wasn't handsome enough, strong enough, athletic enough, handy enough, popular enough, or smart enough, or . . . or . . . or maybe it was his father. Maybe his father was just an ass. Maybe his father was incapable of feeling love. Michael couldn't remember ever being loved by his father.

Michael had always felt that his father resented him, resented having children at all. Maybe that was why his father found so much fault with his children, found so much fault with him.

Fathers were supposed to be wise and kind. Michael expected his father to know those things. How to love and care. How to be a good example. But his father was not. His father was a man who did not want children, a man who did not want responsibility, a man who believed he was always right, a man who did not know how to love. Maybe that was why he was always critical of Michael. Michael couldn't do this correctly; Michael was inadequate at that. According to his father, Michael was wrong in most situations.

It wasn't the apathy that Michael felt from his father that made him angry; it was the systematic destruction of his confidence. The criticism and rejection, the finding of fault, pointing out lack, mentioning incompetence, noticing school marks not made, the failures, the errors, the mistakes, the missteps, the shortcomings, always focusing on these rather than the successes and accomplishments. The message was loud: To his father, Michael was a disappointment.

And maybe the feeling of being a disappointment, the resentment that Michael felt from his father, the constant finding of fault, the constant reminders that he did not measure up, maybe that accumulated attack, the total of that disregard was why Michael found so much fault with his father.

Well, parents are not the only ones that feel disappointment, Michael thought. Michael felt that way about his father too. His father was a disappointment. You're supposed to be the parent, Michael thought. You're supposed to be the person who makes me feel safe. And you did not. You never did. And that made Michael angry. It made Michael angry when he was younger, and it made him angry now.

And that night, that night that solidified the rift in the family, that night, watching his father with his hands all over Beth, that was the moment when Michael drew the line. He knew what his father was, and he knew who his father loved. And from that moment, the distance and the anger grew.

And building the boat. Every moment of the building proved to Michael that his father wanted to get away from him, from them, from his life. And taking mother away, and sailing off, and not calling them, or writing them, and . . . And through it, the anger Michael felt turned to bitterness.

And then leaving Mother, and then divorcing, and then Mother's death. Michael's anger grew at each junction until he thought he would explode. So Michael pretended. He pretended he didn't care. Michael pretended he wasn't hurt.

And then this. This quest, this odd compulsion to find his father . . . to somehow reconnect. Well, he found his father, and he came, and he opened the door, and his father slammed it with a thundering bang, and there was nothing to be done. Michael would go back to the States, back to his family and back to his life, and he would do the best he could to not be angry at his father, but he would be. When he thought of his father, when he thought of this most recent rejection, Michael would be hurt, and he would be angry, and he would pretend he didn't care. Oh well, too bad, he thought, too bad.

Michael completed his meal and headed back to his hotel.

————

———

CHAPTER 49
Beth on the Run

Beth sat in the back seat of the taxi as it raced toward the airport. She tried to put the horrifying dockside experience out of her mind. The burns, the pain, the shock, the stench, the pity. And the memories. The memories she silenced all these years. The memories of her desire for her father. How could she put them back into the darkness, force them to return into her subconscious? How could she keep them out of her mind? She would spoil herself, she thought. That would help. She would go somewhere else before she went home. Somewhere exotic. Someplace where she knew no one. She would go somewhere and buy expensive things. Buying pricey jewelry and clothing would make her feel better. And she would drink. That usually worked. It had to work. It always did the trick before.

Of course, this situation was different. In the storms that followed the discovery that night, she convinced herself that she was the victim. That she was not a catalyst for the happenings of that night, in the living room of the old house, with her father and the table of dust catchers. Somewhere deep at her core, there was a faint whisper that was not true, but the feelings never spoke more loudly than her unconscious dismissal, or ever hit her with the force they did seeing her father being carried away on the dock. Even with the thoughts of her favorite diversions, and the relief of leaving that rattrap minibar hotel, she could not shake the guilt, anxiety and shame she felt.

She tried to reach Michael by phone, but he didn't answer. She couldn't tell him what she remembered, what she remembered about that ridiculous night so long ago, but she could tell him about Father. She could tell him about the fire. She could tell him about the ambulance. Then she would be absolved of that guilt, at least. She would have done something, something so that Father would not go through this alone. It couldn't be her. Father could never know, but she couldn't do nothing. She did not want to live with that. She would kick the responsibility onward, and the guilt could belong to Michael. But she wasn't willing to take the chance that he did not get the message. She had to tell him herself.

As the taxi raced toward her escape, she called several more times, but still there was no answer. And each time he did not answer, she became more and more frantic. Where was he? Was he ignoring her, she wondered? Was her brother not answering his phone on purpose? Was this his way of saying I told you so? He was going to punish her for not believing him. He was going to ignore her. Well, she would not be ignored. She would not be the responsible party. And she would not allow the anxiety to drag on. Instead of going to the airport, she would lead a frontal assault. She ordered the taxi to turn around and gave the confused driver the name of her brother's hotel.

———

CHAPTER 50
The Messenger

Michael left the restaurant in a morass of brooding agitation. He walked through the tourist-perfect streets toward his hotel, but he saw none of the charm, none of the constructed allure of Palma's trendy area. He was angry. He was sullen. He was troubled. For years he suppressed his rage. He hid his hurt with nonchalance. He ignored his embittered past. But now, after trying, after traveling half-way across the world, after reaching out only to receive the same disregard he felt for years, he couldn't stop the volcano that exploded inside. Well, he would forget. He would go back home and put this ridiculous trip behind him. He would let the foolish idea that maybe, just maybe, his father would want to communicate with his son, with his family, scatter on the winds. Michael smoldered through the early evening as he headed back to his lodging. He blistered. He fumed. He burned.

Michael entered the lobby. And there, as he had feared, back like a bad déjà vu, was his sister.

"So, you came back?" Michael asked Beth.

"Yeah, well fuck you too," Beth said.

"I thought you might," Michael said. "That's why I went to dinner. I knew when you got to the harbor, saw the boat, and saw there was nothing for you, no take-away for poor little Beth, you'd have to blame someone. I knew you'd come here and screech at me.

Wail like a harpy. And then after the hysterical raging, you'd leave in a cloud of drama. That's how it has always been, hasn't it, Sis? If it isn't about Beth, it isn't about anything."

Her brother's anger surprised Beth, but she didn't blame him. She understood too well. "It is nice to have someone to be mad at, isn't it?" Beth said in a cynical voice. "Everyone wants someone to be the target of their anger and disappointment, don't they? Look at you. You came here hoping to find the answers to all the questions you have about the past, all those twenty-odd years ago, and instead, you find Poppa drowning, and with him all your hope sinking in the sea. Didn't you want someone to be angry with? You thought you'd find a nice tidy package of resolutions, and suddenly, the mire that is your life would just vanish. You thought you'd go forward inspired and filled with a new lust for the future. Well, it doesn't work that way, Michael. No one gets off that easy. Not you, not me, not him."

Michael exhaled a huge breath and sat on one of the lobby sofas. "I thought Father would have some regret," Michael said in weariness. "Some sense of loss. But there wasn't any."

"You are a chump," Beth said, sitting beside him. "Father doesn't have those kinds of feelings. He doesn't feel the things normal people feel. He is a sociopath. It comes from years of being narcissistic. I know. I recognize the pattern. If you really came here expecting that he would somehow take responsibility for the damage he caused in our lives, then you are hopeless. Father has no feelings. He has no conscience. He has no sense of right and wrong."

"Dad is not a sociopath," Michael said. "He is an eight-year-old boy who has never learned love. He hides his lack of self-esteem by being overblown and cocky. He is Peter Pan. Look at him here, crowing on the pirate ship, living out the won't-grow-up life. He is withdrawn. He lives almost completely in isolation. He ventures out to the local bars where he can play at who he wants to be. The life of the party. The crazy expatriate. And the whole 'book thing,' it is just him searching for approval, for an identity. He wants to feel he is someone, someone special, someone recognized. But the tragedy for him is that there is no one to give him that endorsement. There is no one to offer him the permission he needs to accept himself. Instead, he runs."

"Well, his running days are over for a while," Beth said.

"What do you mean?" Michael asked.

"I left you a message. At the front desk. Did you get it?" Beth inquired.

"No, I was at dinner. What is it?" Michael asked.

Beth steeled herself. "Father was in a boating accident, a fire. I saw him on the dock. He was badly burned," Beth informed. "They were loading him into an ambulance."

"What? Why didn't you tell me?" Michael accused.

"I just did. I tried to call earlier, but you didn't answer, so I left a message with the desk clerk," Beth said in her best don't-blame-me voice.

"Oh, my God. Do you know where they took him? We should go to see if he is all right," Michael said.

"Not we. Not me. Not I," Beth corrected.

"What?" Michael was astonished.

Beth backed away. "I can't . . . I won't . . . I don't want to see him. Especially not under these . . . circumstances."

"You are heartless," Michael said to his sister, his anger returning.

"No," Beth said. "I . . . I . . . What can I do? I'm not a nurse. I can't help him."

"You can be there," Michael insisted, "and make sure he is all right."

"Compassion has never been my forte," Beth responded. Michael's first reaction was annoyance. His sister's selfishness often annoyed him. How could she come to deliver this news and then absolve herself of action? He turned toward her in blind fury, looked at her, and then stopped. Something was different. He couldn't pinpoint it exactly, but there was a change in his sister. She wasn't leaning forward defiantly. Her chin did not thrust forward with the usual dare. There was no compressed sneer on her lips. She was less aggressive, less hostile. Less . . . something.

"What happened?" Michael asked.

"I've told you," Beth repeated, turning away from him. "I went to the harbor. I saw the smoke. I saw the boat. I saw the medics. I saw Father." What she didn't say, what she was thinking, the thought that haunted her, was that she was the one who was responsible. Ultimately. For this. For him. For that night so long ago. For those accusations of molestation. For those years of guilt. She realized it was her. It had been her.

She remembered being in the darkened room on that night. She was sitting. She was waiting, waiting for Father to come home. She knew he would probably be drunk. He was drunk a lot those days. She knew he would feel disoriented. She thought about this for a long time. What it might be like to kiss him, to have him hold her. Maybe she just wanted to feel loved by him again. Maybe that's what she wanted all along. To feel the same as she did on those rare occasions when her father thought she was so special and extraordinary. Somewhere in her mind, she thought that if he held her, if he kissed her, not like a little girl, but like the young woman she had become, then she'd feel all right about herself. She'd feel . . . complete . . . wanted . . . as if she belonged . . . as if she were loved. She waited that night, and when her father knocked into the table and the dust-catchers fell, she stood up, reached out her arms to pull him close to her, and raised her needing mouth to his lips.

She locked that all away in the trauma of the ensuing discovery. She buried those memories in all the anger her mother showed for her father's actions. In all the anger Michael felt. Everyone blamed her father. He was the adult. He was the responsible party, but he wasn't. When she saw him this afternoon on the dock, caretakers lifting the charred body and placing him on a stretcher to race him to the hospital, she remembered the truth. She spent all of her adult life trying to make it be her father. But it wasn't, it was her. She was the instigator. She was the catalyst. She was the cause.

Jonathan, her younger brother, knew. She was certain he saw through the misdirection. There is an advantage in watching from the sidelines, you can see the magician's sleight of hand. He never confronted her about it, but she knew when she looked at him that night, that he saw the truth. And now, now that she was face to face with it once again, she couldn't go. She couldn't see her father. Not in this condition. Not knowing that she wanted her father in that intimate way.

She couldn't tell Michael. And she couldn't live through the guilt, so she was going to do the thing that was the easiest. "I have to go, Michael. I have a plane to catch."

"Then why did you come here?" Michael asked. "Why did you come back here tonight?"

"I wanted to make sure you got the message," Beth said. "I knew you would not want Father to be alone. You still have a heart." Michael stared at her as she grabbed her carry-on and walked to the hotel doors. Michael followed her out onto the street.

"Where are you going?" Michael asked.

"I don't know," Beth said. "I hear Barcelona is nice. There must be some lovely young men there. Some sights to see." She turned to her brother with a plea. "Please, Michael, don't tell Father I was here, okay? Don't tell him I saw his boat. Don't tell him I saw him. Don't tell him I called you." Then she hailed a nearby cab and got into the taxi. The door shut, and the cab drove off into the Majorca night.

Michael went directly to the main desk, retrieved the message, and with the help of the night clerk, discovered where the ambulance took his father. Then he went to the hospital. He didn't know what he would say. He didn't know what he would do. He simply went.

When he arrived and identified himself, he found out his father was in the treatment room, was sedated, and would not regain consciousness until the morning. Damn, he thought, parents can be a lot of effort. At least the say and do were forestalled. He went back to the hotel and drank himself to sleep, thinking, struggling, examining what he wanted to do.

———————

CHAPTER 51
Eyes Opening

When Mac regained consciousness, he was lying in a hospital bed. At first, he was confused. He could only see from one of his eyes. Sight from the other was impeded. He looked down and saw his left hand and arm were covered with gauze. Then he remembered the blaze. He lifted his unbandaged hand and felt his face. All but the square around his right eye were dressed. Well, not all. But most. He wondered how extensive the burns were, but he was too tired to investigate.

"You have returned to the living," the nurse said, checking the patient's blood pressure.

"How did I get here?" Mac asked.

"You were found on the dock. An ambulance was sent. You spent several hours last night in surgery. And now you are here. Are you hungry? Would you like some breakfast?"

"I don't know. I don't think so," Mac said. "Coffee, yes."

The nurse adjusted the bed, set up the hospital tray, and stepped into the hall, returning with a cup of coffee from her cart. She put the coffee on the bed tray and removed the lid. "Can you manage?" the nurse asked.

"Yes, I think so. Thank you." The nurse left to attend to her chores. Mac wasn't hungry but was grateful for the coffee. It wasn't just the taste or the physical effect of the caffeine; coffee was a signal, a marker, a delineation of the day. It served as a frame for what already occurred, and what was to occur. He wondered what his life would be if there was no morning coffee. How would he rally? Fortunately, today, there was no need to find out. There was coffee. Two sips later, there was a knock at the door, and Ernesto poked his head into the room.

"You are sitting up, that is good," Ernesto said. He carried a small vase of flowers, which he set on the nightstand. "My wife. She sends her thoughts."

"She is very kind," Mac said. "Thank her for me."

Ernesto nodded. "I will." He took the nearby chair, pulled it alongside the bed and sat uneasily. "With those bandages, you look like a mummy," Ernesto observed. "So, what happened?"

"The propane tank exploded," Mac said. It surprised him to find that talking hurt. He would have to be succinct. Another first.

"That is the story that is being circulated. I only wondered if it was true. Do you know how many people die in accidents like this? You are lucky to be alive," Ernesto said in wonder. "Think of it, fire, and still you rise. You are like that bird, that phoenix."

"I can tell you, the myth is overrated," Mac said.

"Give it time. Who knows what you will become in a few weeks?" Ernesto quipped.

"If the bird knew he would have to be toasted to live again, he'd have flown the coop," Mac mumbled through the gauze. "How did you know I was here?"

"I have a nephew with the dock patrol." Ernesto's family was everywhere. "The nephew spoke to his cousin, who called his uncle, who is related to my sister by a second husband; of course, I was told. Relatives can sometimes be effective, at least in our small circle. What is the last you remember?"

"The fire. The burning. The extinguisher. The fight. Then nothing."

"One of the nearby boats reported smoke," Ernesto told him. "They came to investigate, but you were miraculously on the dock. They found your dinghy floating near the beach."

"Stupidity," Mac said. "That is what survival instinct really is. Men fight hard to keep moving on, even when it is impossible. I have always thought of endurance as noble, but now I know it is just ignorance."

"Smart or stupid, survival is good. I understand your son came to the boat late yesterday afternoon." Ernesto could see Mac's face cloud even through the bandages. "Was it a good visit?" Ernesto asked.

"No," Mac said. "Looking at the past, revisiting difficult times, knowing you will never see things in the same way as the other does. What is the point? To me, when I left my family, it was escape. To my son, it was desertion. Can those views ever merge?" Mac thought of the meeting from yesterday. It was yesterday, wasn't it? His son, on the deck of the boat, and that smug accusing face, hiding years of anger. More exactly, Mac's mind replayed the memory of the meeting from yesterday; rather the memory of that memory. The meeting echoed a million times even before his son's boat reached the shore. Each remembering was a piece of broken mirror, creating its own specific reflection. In one, you could see freedom; in the other pain. Mac knew that the truth of what occurred was somewhere amid the refractions.

"It is never easy," said Ernesto. "Husband to wife, child to parent, friend to friend, there are no two people who will see exactly the same. None are right, but none are wrong. Together we make time and truth. Life is a kaleidoscope through which we can see great beauty in great chaos. That is what makes the viewing worthwhile. The viewing is worthwhile, my friend, even if it does not always seem so."

A thought came to Mac from his own kaleidoscope. There was something in the way Ernesto spoke. Mac looked at his friend. "Do you think . . . do you think I tried to kill myself?"

Ernesto knew he was on unsteady ground. A person who looks for escape does not like it if they are unsuccessful. "Family reunions can be stressful," Ernesto said.

Mac listened. The question was clear. Mac might have blazed with rage, but the genuine concern of his friend put out that flame faster than the extinguisher had his galley fire. "I did not set the fire intending to have a Viking funeral," Mac said. "I will tell you the truth, my friend, I didn't even think of it. Though, in retrospect, it is a good plan."

"It was my wife who wondered," Ernesto blurted, hoping to clarify that the thought had never entered his mind. That was not the truth. Ernesto did wonder. "She knows how difficult it has been for you. I told her that she was wrong, but I . . . I . . . I can understand how a person experiencing such current challenges might consider the option."

"I promise you, my friend," Mac said, "that if I ever decide to take action, I will have a big party at your café, kiss all the women in town and then sail into the sea. I am not fond of pain."

"Well, good," Ernesto said. "If I am ever to live without your friendship, I will want time to prepare." They talked for several minutes, Ernesto sharing the news of his family and the gossip about the regulars at the café. Mac was happy to have time with his friend but began to tire, so Ernesto left with the promise that he would check-in the next day.

CHAPTER 52
Michael in the Morning

Michael woke the next morning with a splitting headache, the result of bourbon and bad temper. The evening before was a battle for Michael over who he was most angry with, Beth or his father. His father with the years of dismissiveness and abandonment held an early lead, but Beth was gaining ground with her self-centered greed and her insistence to return to Michael's hotel and inform him of their father's accident. Michael felt betrayed by both of them and spent his time vacillating between who most betrayed him. At last, the liquor and the anger took their toll, and he closed his eyes and slept.

Sleep was not gentle. Michael tossed most of the night in fits and starts. Every time he'd fall into sleep, the dream from the plane — his father being consumed by fire — played. But this time, Michael saw himself in the dream. He was standing to the side of the conflagration and watching, not moving. He knew he should call for help. He should sound an alarm or knock his father down and roll him on the ground, but in the dream, Michael did nothing. He only watched. Michael would wake in a drowsy sweat and shake off the images, but when he went back to sleep, the dream would start again, and each time, Michael thought he should do something, take some action, do anything, but he didn't. He just stood there. Watching.

Michael looked at the bedside clock. He needed to get dressed and start moving. His flight was scheduled for that afternoon, and he wanted to go to the hospital to see how his father was. At least, that is what he thought he should do. That was what he had planned, but he wasn't sure he would follow through. Either way, he did not have the luxury of sleeping it off. It was time to get moving. He brewed a strong cup of coffee with the in-room coffee maker and took two aspirins. That would clear his head, even if it did not add clarity to the situation.

Damn Beth, Michael thought. She could have left without a word, and he would have never known what happened. Then Michael could have left, gone to the airport, caught his flight and spent hours thinking how pointless his trip was. He wouldn't have felt guilty; he wouldn't have felt any responsibility at all. He could have turned his back in ignorance and gone on with his life, trying to put his father out of his mind once again. But instead, Beth went out of her way to drop the situation in his lap.

Why? Wouldn't it have been easier for her just to leave? Beth could have pretended she had never witnessed the scene on the dock. It wouldn't be the first time she'd chosen to forget something. She had a history of selective reality. But she didn't leave, and she didn't forget, she came to tell him about the accident. That made Michael wonder what had happened.

Michael could have understood if Beth came back to the hotel to fuss and fume about how wronged she felt. That was an often-heard battle cry. But she didn't. Even Beth's pointing out that Michael's expectations for the trip were unrealistic lacked the verve and insistence of her usual antics.

And then, right before she left, Beth asked Michael not to tell Father that she saw him at the dock. Not to tell Father that she even came to Majorca. Why that? What happened at the harbor? What was it that Michael saw in his sister's face? Was it fear? Concern? Guilt? Maybe seeing Father carried away by the medics dented the shield she wore around her heart.

Beth was right about one thing. She said Michael came to Majorca for a tidy package of answers. It was true. And she said Michael was a chump to believe the situation could have a comfortable resolution. What phrase did she use? "No one gets off that easy." Maybe she was right about that as well. Sitting here in his hotel room, drinking coffee, and deciding what he wanted to do was not easy. Going to the hospital to see his father would not be easy. Not going to the hospital to see his father would not be easy either. He was in an impossible situation because of his sister, and he cursed her for not letting him be.

He didn't know what to do. He felt as immobile as his dream-self. He was angry and anxious and conflicted. He needed someone to talk with. Just to talk it through, a sounding board, a way to see what he really felt, but he didn't know who to call.

His wife wasn't the best choice when it came to the subject of his father. She aligned in sympathy to Michael and reacted like a lioness to any situation that caused her husband unhappiness. His wife lived with Michael's familial feelings for a long time. She did not want him to go to Majorca in the first place. She was certain the trip would not end well. Michael went anyway, and he wasn't certain his wife could be impartial about the situation.

There were friends. A few of them were closer than others, but Michael did not feel safe enough with any of them to share this. He always presented a good face about his family history to the people he knew, much in the same way that his mother dressed and arranged her three children — to create the perfect appearance. He never told any of his acquaintances about his vanishing patriarch or the anger he felt toward his father.

He couldn't imagine calling one of them now and saying, "Hi, I'm in Majorca. Yesterday, I saw my father for the first time in twenty-five years, and he told me that I was basically a disappointment. Then, my crazy sister flew to the island thinking that I was trying to cut her out of an imaginary inheritance. I tried to convince her she was wrong, but she didn't believe me, so she went to the harbor to find our father and arrived just in time to see him being loaded into an ambulance after being pulled out of a fire on his boat. I just wanted to talk to someone about how I felt and see if you could offer any advice about what I should do with an extra crispy parent. By the way, how's the weather back home?"

Besides the ridiculousness of such an intimate conversation with a tee-time buddy, it was nine a.m. in Majorca. It would be the middle of the night in the United States, and no friend, no matter how often you let them win at golf, will welcome having their sleep interrupted.

And it was so early, and it was so late, and he thought that if he didn't talk to someone sane, he would disintegrate, right there in the hotel room. Housekeeping would find a pile of ashes on the floor, and though there was a certain poetic symmetry between his decomposing to ash and his father's new status as a burn victim, Michael was compelled to do something. Finally, he picked up his cell phone and dialed the only number he could think to call.

After four rings, a husky, sleep-laden voice answered, "Hello?"

"Robert, this is Michael, Jonathan's brother. I am sorry to call in the middle of the night like this, but there has been an accident."

"An accident?"

"Yes, can I talk to Jonathan?"

"Of course, hold on." Michael could hear the muffled sounds of Robert rousing his partner. "It's your brother. There's been an accident."

"Michael?" Jonathan said, taking the phone. "Are you all right?"

"Yes. No. I don't know. I'm sorry to call."

"It's all right," Jonathan assured Michael. "What's going on?"

"It's Father," Michael reported. "He's been in an accident."

Jonathan's heart tightened. "What sort of accident?"

"There was a fire on his boat."

"Oh, no. Are you still in Majorca?"

"Did Beth tell you?"

"She mentioned it," Jonathan said.

"Trying to recruit an ally, I bet."

"Beth always campaigns for support. She told me she might fly there."

"Yes. Non-stop and first class, I'm sure. Did she pitch the idea of Dad stashing cash?"

"I told her I wasn't interested," Jonathan said.

"Well, that didn't stop her. I went to the boat to find Father earlier that afternoon. It was not a joyous reunion. Then Beth showed up at my hotel with that hysterical delusion. When she went to the harbor to confront Father, she saw a lingering cloud of smoke hovering above his boat, and the medics were loading Father into an

225

ambulance. They took him to a local hospital where they are treating him for extensive burns."

"Oh, no. How awful," Jonathan said. Michael could hear Robert in the background asking what happened. Jonathan gave him a capsulated report. "Father has been badly burned in a boating fire." Jonathan returned his attention to Michael. "How is he? Have you seen him?"

"I went to the hospital last night, but Father was sedated, and they would not allow me visit. I plan to go there this morning on my way to the airport."

"I assume Beth is not going with you."

"She left Majorca last night after dropping the bomb. She was strange, she asked me not to tell Father she saw him."

"I'm sure it was a terrible shock," Jonathan said.

"It's something more," said Michael. "Something happened when she saw him. She was rattled when she came back to my hotel after, but she wouldn't tell me what happened. I don't understand."

Jonathan understood. Jonathan knew that Beth was in love with her father. Not like a daughter, but sexually. Maybe she only wanted Father's approval. Maybe she was competing with Mother. Maybe a daughter who does not feel a father's love will use any available ploy. Jonathan did not know the reason, but he knew how Beth felt. Jonathan watched.

At first, Beth was coquettish toward her father. Smiling, giggling, flashing those "show-me-how-cute-I-am" eyes. Then as Beth got older, Jonathan noticed that she would find reasons to touch Father in a way that seemed odd. Hugs with hands that stroked his back, kisses on the cheek that seemed intimate, embraces that lasted a little too long. And as she reached puberty, he could see her desire grow. Most girls he knew at that age shifted their attentions to a boy at school or one in the neighborhood, but Beth did not. Beth always got what she wanted by fixating on the outcome with laser focus. Jonathan saw that Beth fixed her laser on Father. And so, Jonathan watched his sister in the weeks leading up to that night.

He saw the plan forming in Beth's head. He noted her preparation. He discovered her sitting in the darkness that night. He observed her moving the end table forward a few inches. It was only a few inches, but it was just enough to impede the familiar path. He witnessed her practicing to stand for an embrace. He heard Father's car drive up to the house, and he heard the key in the front door. That was when he realized what was about to happen.

Maybe he should have shouted out. Maybe he should have tried to disarm her. Maybe he should have stopped it in some way. He might have saved them all from the guilt and the alienation. Maybe he should have stepped forward. Maybe he should have told the family what he suspected after they accused Father. But he didn't. Secrets are curious things, he thought. The longer you keep them, the more difficult they become to tell.

Jonathan wanted to tell Michael what he knew happened that night so long ago. But what good would it do now? The time for action was before. He let that moment pass, and then . . . the encounter happened, and the trajectory of their family altered. He told himself there was no evidence, only what he thought he saw. Only what he thought he felt. Only what he thought he knew. But he knew. It must have been gut-wrenching for Beth to see the man she had loved in such a vulnerable state.

"How can I help?" Jonathan asked.

"I don't know. I came here to, I don't know, to yell at Father, I think. I found some old photos in a closet. Some were from a family get-together when we were kids. I thought they'd all been destroyed, but when I found those pictures, I don't know, all those feelings came back. I tried not to think about him, about all that. But I couldn't stop it. And the more I thought about that life, the angrier I became. Do you remember? Nothing really got settled. He just sailed away with Mom. And I guess I wanted to see him, to finish things. I tracked him down and traced him to here.

"At first, I didn't know what I'd do if he was found. Maybe I would have tried to forget it all again, but then, when he was located, I decided that was it. I was coming to exorcise the past. You know, some closure. Not just about Beth, but about everything. I wanted to tell him how angry I was back then about the way he treated us, treated me. And then I realized that I was still angry. I thought Father might be sorry, but when I saw him, he wasn't. And that made me angry again. And I don't know, I just don't want it to haunt me anymore." Michael took a deep breath. Silence filled the line.

"Fathers pin a lot of hope on their children," Jonathan said after a moment. "Beth escaped by gender. And it was apparent from early on, that I was not going to fit into the norm, so Father focused on you. I am so sorry."

"I feel like I am twelve years old again," Michael said.

"I know. A part of us freezes at the age we are when we feel we are not loved," Jonathan said.

"And now, with this," Michael said, "with this accident, I don't know what to do. Do I go to the hospital and tell him how terrible he was to me? Do I tell him how angry I have been for so many years? Do I tell him he's a shit? Do I tell him how sorry I am about the accident and then leave, reminding him to send a card and let us know how the recovery is going?

"And Beth. I am so angry with our dear mess of a sister. I'm irritated she came to Majorca, annoyed she went to the harbor, and enraged she came back to put it all on me. Again. Still. Once more. Once again, I feel I have to be the responsible one, and I want my chance to be selfish. I want to be selfish."

Michael stopped, and there was silence again. He knew Jonathan was searching for the right thing to say. Michael knew his brother would have the magic phrase, the abracadabra, that Michael needed to go to the hospital and make everything better.

"You know, there was a period when I was angry all the time," Jonathan said.

"You? Angry? You were always calm."

"No, I was just hiding. I got a lot of practice hiding," Jonathan said. "I don't think any of us children felt accepted or loved. Our parents were always involved in their own tug of war. Who was right, who was wrong, who did what to whom? It affected all of us, but we handled it in different ways. You achieved. Beth demanded. I went away."

"I always envied you," Michael said, "getting out of the mess."

"Yes, life led me to Robert, but it was a winding journey. I kept finding stand-ins for Father — teachers at college, short-term friends, romances — each of them put me off balance like Father did. They would point out my flaws, or the shortcomings of my ideas. Sometimes, I was hurt by what was said, but I learned to listen because I found there was value in the views they offered.

"Did I ever tell you about the two bums I saw on the Bowery in New York? This is a true story," Jonathan said. "These two bums sat together in the gutter, side by side, each unkempt, probably homeless, and each with a bottle of wine. As I walked by, I heard one say to the other, 'You have no ambition, that's why you'll never amount to anything.' It made me think of home. 'I'm right, and you're wrong, and that makes me better than you.'

"I found myself attracted to people like that, and I'd get caught up in the struggle for power. Then, I met Robert. It wasn't perfect, even at the start. But after the excitement wore off, which was about three weeks in, I started noticing his faults. He was finicky and chatty. He parsed everything I said until I thought I'd scream. He often interrupted me when I was working, and I thought he was selfish." Michael could hear Robert protesting in the background.

"It sounds like our family," Michael said.

"Exactly," Jonathan said. "I wasn't sure Robert and I would make it through that time," Jonathan continued. "I remember we had a big fight — well a loud discussion, a very loud discussion — and he said something like, 'Well, what did you expect? Did you think I would be what I wasn't for you?' And then I realized that is exactly what I expected. That's pretty unfair, don't you think?

"When I let go of my expectations, he underwent a metamorphosis. His being finicky turned to a careful attention to detail. His chattiness became companionship. And his interruptions, although not always well-timed, I saw as love. It's amazing how quickly a person can change when you look at them from a different point of view."

"Are you saying I should see Father that way?"

"I don't know what you should do, but I wonder what you would feel if you thought of Father differently? What if he loved us in the only way he knew? What if his criticism and withdrawal were only his feelings of being inadequate? Maybe it wasn't about you, or me, or even Beth. Maybe it was him. Maybe it was all he knew."

"But I am angry," Michael said.

"So, go and scream. Tell him he was terrible to you. Rant, rave, and carry on until you have had enough. See if you feel better."

Michael knew he wouldn't. As long as he wanted something from his father, he would be angry. "So, what do I do?" Michael asked.

"Anger is an overpacked suitcase. It takes a lot of effort to carry it around."

"Put it down," Michael said.

"Hasn't it been enough? It was for me. After the change with Robert, I started to see our family differently. Parents, siblings, we're all just sailing together. Each does the best they know. When I saw our parents differently, just as I did with Robert, I stopped being angry. I put down the suitcase. It was too much work."

"You make it sound easy," Michael said.

"I don't know about easy," Jonathan offered, "but there was no return for all my anger except my unhappiness. What is the old saying? 'Holding onto anger is like drinking poison and expecting the other person to die.'"

Michael understood, at least in theory. Jonathan was a kinder soul than his brother.

"Tell Father that if he needs anything, Robert and I will help. He can come here to recuperate, if he wants, with no expectation. He can stay as long as he cares to, and he can leave when he wants. Michael, remember, you are not alone."

"There is one thing that struck me last evening," Michael said. "I didn't think of it before. Why didn't Beth stop Father? All those

231

nights ago. Why didn't she yell out, or knee him in the groin? I know it surprised her, but why didn't she do something?"

"Hmm. That is an interesting question. You'll have to ask Beth."

Michael thanked Jonathan for the ear, then said his goodbye. He still wanted to shout at his father, and maybe he would. He'd find out when he got to the hospital. He got dressed, packed, and picked up his suitcase to leave. It was heavy.

———

———

CHAPTER 53
God at Sea

Mac drifted in and out of consciousness with only a vague recollection of attending nurses. Somewhere in his stream, he heard "first and second-degree burns," the possibility of some "skin grafting," "many weeks for recovery," and "how lucky he had been." He didn't feel lucky, he had thought. He felt burned and blistered and anguished, then he faded into the diversion of darkness again.

He stirred from his haze when he felt someone at his bedside and was surprised to see a man dressed in black sitting with a rosary in his hand. As he came to a stopping point in his prayer, the man looked up and saw that Mac was awake.

"Hello," said the man.

"Did I die?" Mac asked.

"Not that I know of" said the man. "If you did, no one has yet informed me. That would put the entire reputation of this hospital under scrutiny. What would it be if a patient were to die here, and no one knew? That would not be good. Curious, indeed. I am happy to report that almost never happens at this hospital. If someone dies, they nearly always call me to report the news. I have not received any such news about you, so I can safely assume you are not dead. I'm Father Ramos," the man continued. "I am the hospital chaplain. How are you feeling?"

"Relieved," Mac said. "A chaplain is better to see than the Angel of Death."

"You have a sense of humor. That is good after such a terrible accident," the priest said. "That will help with the healing. I came to see if you needed anything."

"Like a ham on rye?"

"I have never considered a career as a sandwich delivery person. What does that pay? Perhaps I will look into it. Maybe I could combine the two. I could deliver a bocata and a blessing. That may increase business. Actually, I am making my rounds and was wondering if there is anything you want to confess?" the priest went on.

"Do I look like a sinner?" Mac asked.

"I don't judge. I just give an ear," Father Ramos answered.

"You don't have that much time, Father," Mac quipped

"God would listen to a condensed version if you'd like. You could hit the highlights and let Him fill in the rest," the priest said, nodding toward the heavens.

"I am sorry, Father, I don't believe in God," Mac confessed.

"That doesn't matter, God believes in you."

Mac abandoned faith years ago. He couldn't remember exactly when; he just stopped believing. When did that happened? When his mother told him she wished he hadn't come along? Was it when he lost all of his money in a gambling spin? When there was no payoff for his work? When his children hated him? It is hard to believe in God when so much goes wrong. It isn't one incident that causes the belief to disappear. It is the continuing series of them. The continuing saga of hope disappearing. Oh, yes, he could chart the course. The points were easy to plot. He understood why he didn't believe in God, but he didn't understand the reverse. He didn't understand why God believed in him. "Why?" he asked the priest. "Why does God believe in me?"

"Because He loves you," the priest responded.

"How can he love me?" Mac asked. "We've never met. We don't telephone. He doesn't visit. How can he love me?"

"It is his way. He is only love. All that is created is love. He is the Father; we are His children. The Father loves his children."

"I don't see how that can be. Not all fathers love their children," Mac said.

"Yes, they do," Father Ramos said. "Sometimes a father may not like the choice a child makes, but that does not mean the parent loves the child less. With love, in time, the parent will understand. The same is true for the child. In time, with love, the child will understand the parent. It is destiny. All comes from the same source, spirit. Spirit is love. As the source is love, so must be the issue. If there is any thought that it is not love, it must come from the self. What you see in any moment is the reflection of what you are. If we do not see love, perhaps it is ourselves we must love." Mac looked perplexed for a moment, and the priest continued. "You know love, don't you?"

Did Mac know love? He thought. He reached into his consciousness. He could recall many feelings. He was not sure if love was one of them. "I don't know," he said after a moment. "The start of the day often fills me with hope. Company and comradery make loneliness endurable. Romance and passion, those things I know. But love? I am not certain. I think I have always dreamed of love that did not come with a cost. Love given freely. I think I have looked for that for many years. But there has always been the give for the get. You concede to the need and discover the gift has expensive strings.

"There was one day," Mac said, "on the bow of the boat that has become my home, in the middle of the sea, without land on any horizon, watching, suddenly I thought, 'This is what life is. This is all I want. I am satisfied.' But then a storm came up, and the boat was battered, and I thought — make up your mind. How can there be such bliss followed by such trial?"

"You are here," the priest said. "That is love."

"I am burnt and in pain."

"That will pass. The love will remain," the priest said. And then, despite Mac's protests, Father Ramos offered a blessing for Mac's healing and continued with his rounds. Well, hell, Mac thought, if it was that simple, we'd all be happy, and then he drifted back into sleep.

Once again, he was in that beautiful moment of serenity where he discovered what he believed was love. The tranquil waters, the gentle sky, the wonder of being at peace. Then the storm came, pelting him with rain and tossing him on the whims of the waves. The fierce lightning and howling winds, the fear of drowning, the greater fear of losing all he owned, overwhelmed him. He tied himself to the helm, cursed at the sky, and prayed for safety. But there was no relief. The storm continued as he sailed into its center. In his dream, he stood stalwart and sang through the rage. In his memory, he was fearless. In his retelling, he was heroic. In fact, he got drunk and cried. He screamed out, "Fuck you, fuck you," over and over again. He woke himself at that moment and lifted himself once again to the present. When his mind focused, and his eyesight found its way through the haze, he saw his son was standing at the side of the hospital bed.

————————

———

CHAPTER 54
Visitor

When Michael arrived at the hospital that morning, his father was sleeping. Michael thought he was prepared for the visit, but as he walked into the room, he stopped in surprise in the doorway. His father lay in the bed, but it wasn't the father he knew. The father he knew was full of piss and pride. The man in the bed looked weary and frail and was wrapped from head to torso in bandages. The fire. The burning. The Inferno. Michael couldn't imagine what that felt like. He tried to comprehend the effort it took to make it out of the boat and back to shore. To face the possibility of death. To lay here now.

In his mind he had an odd echo. The father in the hospital bed, the son at the door to the room — two men as they moved through life. One day, before long, before too many years went by, he would replace his father. Michael would lay in the bed struggling with the temporal. His son would stand in the doorway watching, waiting. The past, the present, the future in one crystallized moment.

Michael put down his suitcase, placed his jacket and hat on the visitor's chair, and stood thinking of the night before. Beth was so distracted when she returned from the dock. Seeing his father as he was now, he could understand how she would be unnerved, but Michael had the sense there was more to it. Something happened when she saw Father. It wasn't like Beth to give up and run away.

Never. She was the type of person who would dig in her claws and fight to be right, even if she was not. But last night she didn't. Last night she was different, and Michael wondered what caused the change in his sister. Some part of the self-centered, blaming, and insistently dramatic woman, he knew since childhood, wasn't there last night. And then, her asking Michael not to tell Father that she was there, was unusual. The sister he knew would be more likely to insist that he tell their father that she flew all the way around the world, with a great deal of inconvenience and suffering, only to be disappointed once again. But she didn't. What happened? What did she see, what did she think, what did she feel that made her leave?

Michael looked back at the bed. The body stirred. If Michael wanted to run, to pretend he hadn't come here, then he should go. There was a part of him that wanted to dash down the corridor and back to the life he knew as quickly as possible. And he almost did, but the man in the bed moved. Mac's eye fluttered open and he focused on his visitor.

Waking through the haze and gauze of bandages was an odd sensation for Mac. At first, he was aware only that there was someone in the room. Then his vision adjusted, and he saw his son at the side of his bed.

"Michael. How do I look?" asked Mac.

"Alive."

"Well, no one is perfect. What are you doing here? Didn't you have a flight to catch?"

"I was waiting in the airport, when I heard the page," Michael lied. "It was a call from the hospital. They told me you had an accident. Some sort of fire."

"The hospital called? Why? I did not ask them to phone you."

"I was pretty certain you did not list me as the emergency contact," Michael said. "But somehow they found me. Who even knew I was in Majorca? Your bar buddy maybe?"

Leave it to Ernesto, Mac thought. Most likely when Ernesto heard the news of the fire, he called the hospital and told them that Mac's son was in Palma. The hospital must have tracked Michael down. He'd have to remember to give his friend a scolding. People like to meddle, Mac thought. Everybody wants to fix. Everybody wants to put their nose in. They think they are doing a good thing, that they are showing care, but often caring is just doing nothing. There is something about letting things be that is counterintuitive to the nature of mankind.

Father and son were silent for several moments, each waiting, each delaying, each assessing just as they had on the deck of the boat the day before. Mac wondered why his son came to the hospital. Michael wondered what he was going to say to his father. A long minute passed before Michael spoke, "Are you in a lot of pain?" he asked.

"Not bad for a man who's been seared," Mac said.

Michael chuckled. "You always did that. As far back as I can remember, whenever something terrible happened, you tried to say something funny," Michael said. "Like a bad stand-up comedian."

"Well, you remember what my mother said," Mac replied. "'If you can't say something funny, go kill yourself.'"

"Father, it isn't funny. You could have died," Michael said.

"That could happen any day. A fall, a storm, a tourist on a Vespa."

"Ha. Ha."

"It was a propane tank accident. They are not uncommon on sailing vessels. At least the head didn't explode. That would have been real shit."

"And another joke." Michael sighed. He was quiet for a moment. Michael wrestled most of the previous evening with what he would say, what he would do. There was a part of him that wanted to let things be, but there was a part of him that suffered like all of mankind, that wanted to fix, to care. Finally, Michael took a deep breath and stepped through the looking glass, knowing there was no way back. He spoke. "Father, you can't stay on that boat."

Mac was silent for a moment. He did not like it when people tried to tell him what to do. "That boat is my home," Mac pointed out.

"The boat is falling apart," Michael countered. "The wood is battered. The mast needs to be replaced. The sails have holes. Now the galley is burned, and I am sure that is only the beginning of a list of things that are wrong with it. It is too much for you. It is too much for anyone. You can't stay there. You can't go on this way. You need to let the boat go."

"And then what do I do?" Mac asked. "Do I find a little apartment in the barrio and give scenic tours of the boat? 'Right this way señoras y señores, see the place where I set myself on fire.'"

Michael spent all night thinking about this situation; looking at the options. He looked at what he wanted to do, and he looked at what he thought he should do. It was funny, he thought, how infrequently the two things fall into line. Wouldn't it be nice if they did? Michael had wrestled with the choices until he fell asleep from the alcohol. It was a difficult battle. Even standing here, standing in this room, standing at this bed, standing next to his Father in this condition, the struggle continued. It continued until this moment.

There was a pause, and then Michael said, "Come home." Mac heard the pronouncement as a command and was stunned by Michael's edict. Mac's body stiffened in defiance. Michael knew at once that his tone was aggressive, so he let another moment pass and then restated the idea more quietly as a suggestion. "Come back to the States. I have enough money. We have room. We could build a cottage or find a place nearby. An apartment or a small house. You know, there are excellent retirement communities near. You could see your grandchildren. Spend time with them. Talk to them about your travels. Did you know my oldest girl is having her first baby? Your great-grandchild. Your first great-grandchild. Come home."

"Oh, yes, I am sure your brother and sister would love that."

"I've talked to them both. We agree. We all agree." That was not true. He called his brother, and Jonathan had been ready to help in any way. Beth, of course, he did not call. Michael could not guess how she'd react. Based on her odd behavior last evening, he guessed she'd try avoidance. She'd come around in time, and too bad if she didn't. "You don't have to stay near me. Jonathan and Robert said you are welcome to recover at their place if you'd like."

"Can you see it," Mac said. "Two homosexuals and a pan-fried father rehashing family history. A new sit-com."

"See, there you are again with the jokes. They are just a way to hide, aren't they, Father? To keep from facing the truth. A way to avoid being close. A way to say what you feel without the definitive edge of taking responsibility for hurting. And the laughs can go on, one punchline after another, but they do not change the truth. They only make it harder to see."

"Jokes are funny," Mac added. "Rehashing the past is not so funny."

"We wouldn't need to talk about the past," Michael insisted. "We could — get to know each other all over again. Father, look at you, you almost killed yourself in a fire yesterday. You can't take care of the boat any longer. I know you can't have much money left. You've been wandering for over twenty-five years. You can't sail off to another port. You can't battle another tropical storm. You can't keep running to shore to carry groceries back. It's too much. It is time for you to rest."

Michael presented his case. He was passionate but not emphatic. Mac knew that a lot of what his son had said was true, but he was so shocked that he lay there immobile. Live in America again? Go back to his family? Return to all the things he escaped from? Go there to see the ruins and face the past? Live through the curious stares of people he knew three decades ago? Mac lay there, silent, thinking. There were so many questions; Mac could not think which question to consider first. Finally, he settled on the one that floated to the surface.

"Why?" Mac asked. "Why would you do this? Why did you barge into my life? It has been a long time. Why did you send someone to find me? Why did you fly halfway across the world? Why did you come here today, to this hospital, to see me here, in this bed, tired and injured? Why?"

"I don't know," Michael said. "It was easier to stay angry with you when I was younger. It was a fuel. It was a story with a villain, and you were the bad guy. But I don't want to be angry anymore. Now I want to let the anger go. I don't want to think of my childhood and feel resentment for what did or did not occur. I don't want to

243

carry that burden anymore. It is selfish, but I am setting it down. Here. At this moment. I am putting down all that anger, all that weight. I put it down here, now."

Mac looked at his son and saw that Michael was sincere. Whatever toll the past had taken, Michael was letting it go. Mac wondered if he could do the same, if he should do the same, if he wanted to do the same.

Michael continued. "You did what you believed was the best thing for you to do, out of duty, out of guilt or out of hope. I do not know. No one should judge that. Fine, I understand that. But I am through carrying that weight. And you are my father," Michael said. "Whether it suits us or not, we are connected.

"Our relationship has not been easy. There have been some difficult times. What happened cannot be undone, but time is passing. I don't want the strain anymore. There are times when I put you out of my mind. Times when you are not a part of my life. I may be living in peace, or I may be consumed by all the little things that life takes, I don't know, but then I turn and see a father with his family, or I see an older man walking down the street, or I hear someone saying something, and it all floods back. It rolls over me like a tidal wave. And I am floating, floating on anger and resentment once more. I am not good at floating. I don't have those sea legs, and I do not like to swim. I think if we were ever going to build a bridge, this is the time."

"I am not looking for your forgiveness," Mac said.

"I know," Michael said, "but I am looking for yours." Michael looked at his father in a way Mac could not remember seeing. "I want you to forgive me. Forgive me for all the things I have done to make the divide for the last years. Forgive me for seeing you through the eyes of my expectations and not for the person you are."

Mac was suspicious. What was his son up to, he wondered? He comes all the way from the United States, accuses me of a variety of parental failures, and then asks my forgiveness? What sort of trick was this? Mac considered actions. He could argue. He could defend. He could refute. He could refuse. But why? Mac chose agreement. "Well, you were young and foolish," Mac said. "A lot of people have those afflictions."

Michael inhaled and exhaled deeply, taking a moment to steady himself. He knew it was time. Michael knew the pain ended now, for him at least, if not for his father. "So, do you want to come home?" he asked.

Mac looked at his son through the one unbandaged eye. He looked past the years of estrangement, past the mask of an angry child. Mac looked past the memories of the pain he knew Michael lived through. He looked past a father's failings. Past the choices he had made and the effect they had on those around him. Mac saw past the weariness of an unskilled traveler, past the tentativeness of concern, and past the anger of a difficult reunion, and in that moment, in that one look, Mac felt again what he had that day on the boat. Mac felt as he had that day in the middle of the sea, without land on any horizon, watching the beauty of the sky and the sea. And he felt a curious joy. An odd sense of the balance of life. The peculiar feeling of being at peace. And he wondered, is this love?

Somehow in that moment, in that hospital room, with all the pain in his body and one eye covered by bandages, Mac saw love. He felt love. And he wondered, how is this possible? He had not earned it. It was not a reward for long adventures. He didn't believe you can buy it. You cannot demand it or expect it. The best you can do, he thought, is to recognize it.

Having so little experience in seeing love, Mac understood that recognizing it can be hard. But he knew that recognizing it was easier than accepting it. To accept love, you have to accept yourself. You have to accept that you are worth love. You have to forgive yourself for all the pettiness, for all the dreams, for all the choices you have made. And when you have forgiven yourself, then you can accept. It's a big undertaking, Mac thought, to let go of all the things that you have used to define who you are. Because after them, who will you be? Who is left when you let go of all the anger, the regret, the dreams, and the passions? That is what Mac wondered as he lay bandaged in the hospital after the flight and the fight and the fire.

Moments passed before Mac spoke. When he did, he spoke evenly, and without the emotion he felt. He had had years of hiding his feelings. Of covering them with a joke, or with work, or with extravagance. Only the tear on his face betrayed his heart.

"Dreams are interesting things," Mac said. "The pursuit is everything. When you give up the pursuit, what is left?"

And then, all at once, Michael understood. He thought of his own life, all the choices he had made. The constant cycle of trade-offs; the roads chosen, the doors closed, the opportunities passed. Michael sighed. He looked relieved and saddened and definitely lightened. Then he extended his hand. Mac looked at his son's hand for a moment, then he put his own forward, and they shook. It was the first time they'd touched since before Mac had sailed away all those years ago. And then Michael did the most uncanny thing. He bent down and kissed his father on the forehead. And a tear rolled down. A tear rolled down each of their cheeks. Michael picked up his hat to leave. Mac stopped him.

"Wait. How did you know where I was, I mean where to send Dennis? In the entire world, how did you come to send him to Majorca?"

"I got a letter from a friend of yours in Florida. He wondered if I knew where you were. He said the last time he heard, you were here."

Ah, Mac thought. He remembered sending his friend the postcard. He never thought there would be any connection. "It's good to be thought of," Mac said.

Michael took a card from his wallet and set it on the nightstand. "In case," he said. And then he left.

Mac was alone in the room again. Burned and bandaged. The pain and tenderness of the wounds of his skin reverberated like those of his heart. He thought of his son coming all the way around the world to find him, and his eyes filled again. It was a gift, wasn't it? Michael had given him a gift. To ask forgiveness was a release from at least a portion of Mac's past. That was something, wasn't it? Some bit of freedom. One less regret. Maybe he'd have something to remember now that wasn't regret.

In some way, Mac thought, I gave my son a gift in return; freedom from the burden of an odd and eccentric father. From the duty of caring through dotage. From the task of watching the descent.

Besides, he thought, I have my book to publish; I have to find a new authoress. There are pictures to take, releases to draft. He couldn't wait to write letters to all those publishers who turned down the offering. Ha. What fun that would be.

And what would I do in New Jersey, he wondered? There are taxes, Mac thought, horrible government, no socialized medicine, paltry pensions, bad wine, and no bordellos. How could he look to a future without bordellos? And the samba? He loved to samba. Where would he dance the samba? And what about the sunrises, Mac thought? Oh, yes, they have sunrises in America, but not like the ones here. There are no blue waters to see. There is no golden glow that rises from the cathedral. There is no place he knew where he could privately be a part of sensual chaos. Even on days when there is much to do, thought Mac, and all does not go as hoped, there is still nothing as beautiful as the morning in Majorca.

THE END

———————

About the Author

Vincent Rhomberg has been writing for the theater for over thirty years. His work has been produced in Off-Broadway, regional, summer stock and community theaters. This is his second novel.

Made in the USA
Monee, IL
23 October 2020

45938021R00152